WITCHY WOMAN

Also by Steve Brewer
Lonely Street
Baby Face

To Karen!

STEVE BREWER

Thanks for all your help

WITCHY
WOMAN

& support.

■ ◆ ■

A BUBBA MABRY *Best,*

MYSTERY

A THOMAS · DUNNE BOOK

ST. MARTIN'S PRESS ➤ NEW YORK

Design by Junie Lee

Library of Congress Cataloging-in-Publication Data

Brewer, Steve.
  Witchy woman / by Steve Brewer.
      p.   cm.
  "A Thomas Dunne Book."
  ISBN 0–312–14076–2
  I. Title.
  PS3552.R42135W58   1996
  813'.54—dc20   95–33672

First edition: February 1996
10 9 8 7 6 5 4 3 2 1

To my parents, Pete and Bobbie Brewer, and my in-laws, A. J. and Jeanene Gibbs, who've always been there with their encouragement

As always, special thanks to my wife, Kelly, and to best pal Frank Zoretich: couldn't do it without you

O N E

■ ◆ ■

If you've ever wondered what an ass-whipping is worth, I can tell you my price. Three hundred dollars. Not to do the whipping, you understand. Nobody's ever seemed interested in hiring me for that. Three hundred bucks is how much I charged to take one.

It began, as things often do, with a message on my answering machine. A woman with a voice as soft as old money. She said her name was Kathy Grabow and she had a proposition for me. She left her number. I dialed it so quickly, I practically blistered my Touch-Tone finger.

Don't get me wrong. It wasn't the sultry voice. I've got, for lack of a better term, a girlfriend, and she's about all I can handle. What I didn't have was a client, and I was down to living off the change I'd collected over time in a jar in my closet. I'd gone through the quarters already, and the dimes were about gone. Buying anything with nickels seemed too depressing. And it pissed off the clerks at the 7-Eleven when I had to count them out.

I'd been eating. My girlfriend, Felicia Quattlebaum, sees to

1

that. But I was tired of mooching off her. I needed some money, and I needed it quick, and, though Kathy Grabow didn't know it, I'd jump at anything she offered.

She answered the phone, and we agreed to meet at my place. She seemed a little put off by my business address—I work out of my room at the Desert Breeze Motor Inn on East Central Avenue, Albuquerque's nexus of street crime—but she quickly rejected my suggestion that I come to her home.

In the hour I waited for her, I shaved and spruced up. I hadn't been to the coin laundry lately, not when coins were all I had to survive on, but I found a shirt that would pass the sniff test, and splashed on some Brut to cover any aromas I might've missed.

While I waited for Kathy Grabow, I speculated about what kind of case she might have to offer. A divorce case would be best. Days of loitering in my car, spying on some unfaithful hubby, waiting for him to make his move at a no-tell motel. Or some nice, messy lawsuit, complicated and time-consuming.

When she knocked, I counted to three before I snatched it open, trying not to appear too eager. People don't want to hire private detectives who have too much time on their hands. They want the impression you're busy with a long list of big-name clients. It's tough to keep up that front when you're working out of the Desert Breeze.

Kathy Grabow smelled of cocoa butter. It's one of those scents that can make a man crazy, bringing up instant associations with beaches and bikinis and drinks with paper umbrellas in them. Kathy fit perfectly with those fantasies, tall and leggy and tanned as coppery as the Abe Lincolns in my coin jar. Her blond hair was bleached nearly white by the sun, or maybe with the proper chemicals—it was only June, after all, hardly time to get that much sun, even if you spent every day lounging by the pool. She wore a dazzling white tank dress, sunglasses with gold rims, and sandals with no stockings. Most men would gasp at the sight of such a woman. I saw dollar signs.

"Bubba Mabry?"

"That's me. Come on in."

I shook her manicured hand and led her to the big, musty armchair in the corner. I perched on the edge of the bed, close enough that our knees nearly touched, and asked her how I could be of service. She flashed a nervous smile as white as her dress.

"I have your guarantee this is all strictly confidential?"

"That's what this business is about."

"Okay." She took a deep breath, glanced around my room. "It's my husband."

I immediately put on my sympathetic, concerned look, that practiced expression suitable for hearing about infidelity. But that wasn't where we were headed.

"Marty's been having some problems. It started about a month ago, with a fight."

I nodded understandingly. "What were you fighting about?"

"Oh, *we* weren't fighting about anything. We get along great. Marty got into a fight with another guy."

Time to reconfigure my features. This was no motel stakeout.

"We were in a bar over on the West Mesa, that place where they play salsa music? Marty didn't really want to go, but I sort of insisted. It's a hot place. We danced a lot, had a few drinks. Marty doesn't like to dance because I'm taller than he is and he's self-conscious. But he was being a good sport."

I nodded some more. This was familiar. Felicia likes to dance on occasion. I'd just as soon walk on hot coals.

"When it was time to leave, some drunk got between me and the door, started saying nasty things to me."

Kathy Grabow blushed at the memory, reached up to fluff her bangs with her fingertips.

"Marty couldn't just ignore the guy, even though the guy was

3

much bigger than he is. Marty stepped in between us, started yelling at the drunk, gave him a push. The drunk didn't hesitate. He really clobbered Marty. The bouncers jumped on him and dragged him out of the bar, but Marty was on the floor, rolling around and, well, and *crying*. Not that anyone else wouldn't have done the same thing. He was hurt. I had to take him to the emergency room and get his head x-rayed."

"He's okay now?"

"Oh, yeah, he's fine—physically. But it did something to his head. It made him feel like less of a man because he got beat up and I was there to see it."

I shrugged. "The guy took him off guard."

"I know! That's what *I* said. But Marty's acted strange ever since. You'd have to know Marty to understand. He's a little guy, short. He was always the one who got picked on in school. They called him Marty Grabass."

I managed not to grin.

"As he got older, and it became clear he wasn't getting any bigger, he tried to compensate for it in other ways. He took over his dad's construction business after college and turned it into a real moneymaker."

I felt myself salivating and swallowed inconspicuously.

"He married me partly because he was trying to prove something. Don't get me wrong. We love each other. We've been married six years, and it's been great. He takes very good care of me. But there's always a little something of that past there. He tries too hard to make sure he's the big man."

"It's a common affliction." I sat up straight, wiped my sweaty palms on the knees of my jeans. "What makes you think he won't just get over his funk?"

"It's more than just a funk. Marty hired this guy Clyde, a real rough man, and, as near as I can tell, Clyde doesn't do anything but hang around the construction office. He's like one of those big, mean dogs people get for protection. I'm worried Clyde will get Marty mixed up in something criminal."

"Sounds like we need to get rid of Clyde. Is that what you have in mind?"

Kathy Grabow blushed again.

"Not exactly. The problem goes deeper than that. Marty's always been a tiger in the bedroom. And since he got beat up, he's, well, he's had some manhood problems. Do I have to say any more?"

"Not at all. I get you."

"Anyhow, that's how I know this is really bothering him still. And it's why I came to you."

"What do you want me to do?"

"I want you to pick a fight with him. And lose."

Just when you think you've heard it all in this business, something like this comes along. She asked me how much I'd charge her. I did some quick mental calculations, and came up with three hundred bucks. That would be enough to feed me for a couple of weeks and still cover the rent on the first of July. Surely, by then, I could come up with some real investigative work.

She didn't flinch at the figure, just reached into her purse and started writing me a check. I suppose I could've milked her for more, but who knew? I didn't want to price myself out of the market. Probably plenty of guys would take a fall for less.

"If you get hurt," she said, "and need to see a doctor, I'll pay for that, too."

That hadn't occurred to me. I opened my mouth to demur, but she added, "I don't guess that's very likely, though. Marty's not much of a fighter. But he needs to think he is."

We made the arrangements. She was taking Marty to the Town House, a steak joint not far from where I live, that very night. I was to hang around outside around nine o'clock, watch for them to leave, then accost them.

5

"You got any suggestions on how I should provoke this?"

"You'll think of something," she said, "but it would be best if it involved me. You know, say something suggestive to me or something like that. That way, Marty can feel like he's defending my honor."

Saying something suggestive to a virtual stranger was such an alien concept to a well-bred southern boy like me that it made me queasy to think about it. But I had four or five hours. I'd come up with something.

Kathy Grabow rose to leave. "Oh, one more thing. Don't let him win too easily. Make it look good. This is really important."

I promised and showed her to the door.

So that's how I found myself loitering outside the Town House after the sun went down. I was nervous, hoping some restaurant employee wouldn't spot me lurking in the shadows and call the cops to have me booted out of the parking lot.

Kathy kept Marty right on schedule. At nine on the dot, the door swung open, spilling light and the happy couple into the parking lot.

She still wore the tight white dress, and Marty was dressed in a white shirt and khaki pants. Very summery, very wealthy, both glittering with gold jewelry here and there. Marty only came up to her shoulder. He was dark and pudgy, with a wide butt from spending all his time at a desk. They were having a great time. He had his arm around her waist and they were laughing at some private joke, and it seemed terribly rude to interrupt. But I pushed myself out of the shadows and cut them off before they could reach their glimmering BMW. Marty already had his keys in his hand. He saw me, took me for some street beggar, started shaking his head. That somehow made it easier to do what I had to do.

"Hey, baby," I said to Kathy, a little loud, a little slurry so he'd think I was drunk. "Why don't you dump this little shit and you and me will go have some fun?"

Marty bristled immediately. He squared off to face me, standing in front of Kathy and dropping his keys back into his pocket.

"What did you say?"

"I wasn't talking to you, peanut. I'm talking to that good-looking woman there."

"That's my wife, asshole. Now back off."

Very good. Marty was playing his role beautifully, without even knowing it.

"Back off? You gonna make me back off?"

"If I have to." Marty's hands had been loose at his sides, but he suddenly put up his dukes to chest height—waist height on me. I'd have to protect my jewels.

I reached out and jabbed his chest with my index finger. "You sawed-off little—"

Bap!

I didn't get to finish my well-rehearsed insult. Marty surprised me with an overhand right that connected beautifully to the bony socket around my left eye. I didn't see the punch coming, just the lights that flashed in my head.

I staggered backward, getting my hands up to protect myself, trying to make sure I was pointed in the right direction. Marty was all over me, his masculine insecurities landing to my stomach, my forearms, the side of my head. I swung blindly a couple of times, trying to keep my fists low so I'd hit him in his squat body rather than accidentally taking off his head.

I could see better now, saw a nice left hook coming at my jaw. I jerked my head back just enough that I didn't take the full force of it, and went down. My butt hit the asphalt first, and I toppled over onto my side. Marty stood over me like a pint-sized Gary Cooper, his fists still up, his breath coming hard. I didn't try to appear unconscious. I had to keep my eyes open for what I felt sure was coming next.

Marty kicked me in the stomach. I saw it coming and tightened up, but my stomach muscles aren't what they used to be, and it knocked the wind out of me.

"Marty! That's enough!" Kathy grabbed his arm and swung him around. "My God, Marty, you could've killed him!"

Marty beamed at the thought. Then he put his mean face back on to say a final word to me.

"Maybe that'll teach you to mind your manners around a lady."

Kathy clutched his arm and pulled him toward the car.

"Marty! I've never seen you like that. You were wonderful!"

I lay on the ground, watching them. Marty's shoulders were thrown back and his chest was puffed out, and it was my guess the tiger would be back in the bedroom tonight.

T W O

■ ◆ ■

As shiners go, mine was a beauty: puffy and purple and circling from my eyebrow to my nose. I spent much of the next morning standing in front of the mirror in my bathroom, examining the bruise, gently prodding it with my fingertips. It throbbed.

I had a couple of light bruises on my ribs and one elbow was scraped from contact with the asphalt, but otherwise I was fine. Just this purple beacon on my face that said, Hey, everybody! Somebody punched my lights out!

I stayed indoors all morning, sipping Old Charter and flicking through channels on TV. Kathy Grabow's check sat on my bedside table, propped up against the lamp so I could see it and feel better.

She called me around lunchtime, gushing over what a good job I'd done.

"Oh, Mr. Mabry, you were beautiful, just beautiful. Marty could hardly go to sleep last night. He couldn't stop talking about it. When he went off to work this morning, his feet barely touched the ground."

"I'm glad to hear it worked."

"It was just great. But I thought I'd better call and check on you. It looked like some of those punches landed pretty hard."

"He caught me by surprise with that first one, and I've got a black eye. But it's nothing two aspirin can't fix."

Plus, I thought, I've had black eyes before, without three hundred dollars to show for them.

She thanked me some more, then said good-bye. I hung up, stood, stretched, went over to the window to peer out around the curtains. It was a typical Albuquerque summer day, hot and dry and still, with a sky as blue and deep as a sea. Waves of heat shimmered off the asphalt parking lot that occupied the center of the Desert Breeze compound.

You should be out there, I told myself. Enjoying the sunshine. Cashing Kathy Grabow's check. Hustling up some new clients.

I took a nap.

The telephone woke me. I snatched up the receiver, bumping my shiner as I groped to get the phone to my ear.

"Ow!"

"Hello?" It was Felicia.

"Oh, hi."

"Are you all right?"

"Yeah, I just sort of missed my ear with the phone."

"Were you asleep?"

"No, I was just, uh . . ."

"You were asleep."

Felicia doesn't think much of what I do for a living, and she makes few attempts to hide her feelings. Even so, my propensity for napping instead of working irks her.

"I had a job that kept me up late last night," I said quickly. "I was just catching up."

"A job, huh? That's good news, I guess."

"Yeah. Just a little job, a one-night thing. But I made three hundred bucks."

"Good for you. Guess that means you can take me out to dinner."

"Dinner?"

I squirmed around to look at my alarm clock. It was nearly five. The banks were closed. Kathy Grabow's uncashed check stared back at me from the bedside table.

"Oh hell. I didn't make it to the bank."

"Mm-hmm."

"We can still go out. I think I've got a credit card around here that isn't maxed out."

"Don't worry about it. I'll buy. I've had a rough day, and I could use some company."

"Rough, huh?"

"Just the usual. Fighting with an editor who wouldn't know a good story if he bumped into it with his white cane."

She said this last loudly enough to be overheard at neighboring desks. Felicia isn't shy about her opinions. From all accounts, she's the Terror of the City Desk down at the *Albuquerque Gazette*, and proud of it.

We agreed to meet at Baca's at six, and she hung up. Baca's is a forty-year-old Mexican joint, the first place Felicia and I ever dined together. Since that first meal, well over a year ago now, Felicia and I have written an extremely unsuccessful book together, lived together for a while, lived separately. We've been through a few romantic crises, had some good times. She's become such an integral part of my life that it's hard to remember the times before, when I didn't have this smart, irritable little woman pushing me around.

Felicia has a sign on her desk at the *Gazette* that says, FIFTY-ONE PERCENT SWEETHEART, FORTY-NINE PERCENT BITCH. DON'T PUSH IT.

That's a pretty good summation, and a fair warning.

I took a shower, shaved, combed my thinning brown hair. In one of her sweetheart moments, Felicia once told me she likes bald men. She must like me better all the time.

It took me five minutes to get going once I reached my car. A twenty-year-old Chevy Nova, the car is getting more temperamental with age. Downright cranky, in fact. Lately, I have to hold the gas pedal down precisely half an inch while turning the ignition. Any less, the engine simply groans. Any more, it floods out and I have to wait for it to swallow its gasoline before trying to start it again.

It could swallow money as well, if I had any to pour into it. The tires are bald. The muffler's shot. The paint, once a shiny powder blue, has worn through in places, showing the gray primer beneath and the first brown rivulets of rust. If I let the paint job go much longer, it'll look like military camouflage.

In a way, it's already camouflaged. It's the kind of car nobody would look at twice, which makes it perfect for my line of work. And I don't have to worry about anyone stealing it.

But I know it won't last forever. I need it to work, but I can't seem to get enough work to afford the repairs. It's one of those ugly little paradoxes that make life uneasy.

I steered the Chevy into westbound traffic on Central, kept to the slow lane as the engine warmed up, sputtering along. Central's the old Route 66, the major artery through the city. The section of Central where I live, roughly bounded by the Sandia Mountains on the east and the Yuppie shops and cafés of Nob Hill on the west, is known as the Cruise. It's a rough zone of cheap motels and porno shops, prostitutes and petty crooks. It attracts more cops per square mile than any other neighborhood in the city, and it still has the highest crime rate.

I've lived along the Cruise for more than a decade, since I mustered out of nearby Kirtland Air Force Base and decided to stay in Albuquerque. I was attracted to the dry climate and the wide-open spaces, though I've found over the years that I rarely leave the city limits. Wide-open spaces are fine to look at, but when you get out there in them, there's not much to do.

Along the Cruise, there's always something to do, something to see: the latest in hooker fashion decorating the corners; muttering street crazies shambling along with their shopping carts; drug dealers and clients disappearing into alleys for quick transactions. It's cheap entertainment, trying to keep up with everybody's comings and goings.

Felicia won't have anything to do with the Cruise. She got her fill when she stayed with me and we wrote the book together. About the nearest she'll come is Baca's, which is well insulated from the crime zone by the six blocks of gentrified Nob Hill.

Her brown Toyota was in the parking lot when I arrived, and I hurried in, to find her in a vinyl booth just inside the oaken front door. The back half of Baca's, the lounge, features red wallpaper and giant murals and the gaudiest bar in North America, but Felicia had chosen the more subdued front area. She sat in the smoking section, puffing away, a margarita at her elbow.

She looked up as I approached, and her hawklike reporter's eyes went directly to my shiner.

"What happened to you?"

My hand went to the bruise automatically, sending a throb to my temple. I winced.

"I fell out of bed."

"Yeah, right."

I slid into the booth opposite her.

"I got popped last night while I was working."

"Somebody catch you peeking in their window?"

"Not exactly. My client's husband. Lucky punch."

One eyebrow arched above her square glasses like a question mark.

13

"No, I wasn't messing around with my client. It was more complicated than that."

I gave her a brief rundown of what had happened, skipping the names of those involved. My confidentiality pledge forbids revealing identities to newspaper reporters, even if the reporter happens to be my sweetie. Felicia understands that—most of the time.

"So, anyway," I concluded, "he caught me off guard with the first punch. And I got this black eye."

She stabbed out her cigarette, gave me one of her patented "I can't believe what an idiot you are" looks, and said, "You were picking a fight with the guy, and he caught you off guard?"

"I've already got a shiner. I don't need my ego bruised, too."

"All right, Bubba, I'll drop it. I just can't believe you sometimes. You'll take money to be a human punching bag before you'd get a real job."

"If I had a real job, I wouldn't have all these exciting adventures to tell you about."

"I don't know about that. I've got a real job, and I seem to get all the excitement I can handle."

A waitress wearing a totem pole of lacquered black tresses appeared at our table, temporarily forestalling the latest diatribe against Felicia's bosses. We ordered our usual—a combination platter for me, enchiladas for Felicia—and I requested a Carta Blanca. I could've gone for a margarita or three, but Felicia was buying and I didn't want to seem piggish.

The waitress brought chips and salsa to keep our appetites appeased, along with my beer, and I gave Felicia her opening.

"So, you had a rough day, huh?"

She lit another cigarette, huffed the smoke toward the ceiling.

"More of the same," she said. "I've got a terrific story hanging fire, and that idiot Whitworth wants me to spend all my time rewriting press releases and covering meetings."

Whitworth was the city editor at the *Albuquerque Gazette*, a goateed half-pint whose main goal in life seems to be making Felicia's life miserable. At least that's her version. Felicia has some very strong ideas about journalism. When she first came to Albuquerque, she was working as an editor for a celebrity tabloid out of Florida, making big bucks to snoop into the empty lives of the rich and famous. It was teeth-bared, no-holds-barred newspapering, a far cry from the cautious Establishment journalism they practice at the *Gazette*. She'd never adjusted to the difference, and the result was that she spent most of her workdays at odds with those around her.

She described the latest set-to, and I feigned intense interest, though, in truth, it was hard to follow the details over my own crunching. I had eaten little all day, and the warm chips and spicy salsa hit the spot.

Felicia's project involved some sort of land grab on the West Mesa, the fastest-growing part of the city, where scrubby desert gave way daily to ticky-tacky houses that all looked the same. Apparently, the governor was involved in some way that would profit him. No surprise there. In the Third World politics of New Mexico, election victors are expected to take some spoils. And not much business gets done unless somebody in the capital is directly involved.

"The Goddess is pals with the governor," Felicia said, "so I think the kibosh is coming from the very top."

"The Goddess?"

"Mrs. Ogletroop. The publisher?"

"Oh, right. Why do you call her the Goddess?"

"Everybody calls her that. She's like those goddesses in mythology. You never see her, but she exerts her will over you. And she must be immortal, because she's been running the paper for generations without dying off and letting someone with new ideas take over."

The food arrived, all greasy and cheesy, and kept our mouths busy for a while. Felicia seemed mollified, now that she'd had a chance to vent, and we talked about other things between bites. Felicia's pretty when she's not scowling—big dark eyes behind those severe glasses, an oval face that ends in a pointed chin, perfect pink lips—and it gives me great pleasure just to watch her talk. She's short and compact, but with a great body she keeps mostly hidden under slouchy masculine clothes. The thought of that body gave me a tickle in my belly, but she found another topic that made her scowl, and my lust drifted away like so much smoke.

Her parents were talking about coming for a visit. Nothing so terrible there. She got along with them fine, spent an hour every Sunday on the phone with her mom. But they had trouble understanding why she'd dumped a good-paying career to move to the Wild West. Her parents were retired, lived in their native Indiana, and had never been to New Mexico. To them, anything west of Kansas City and east of California was all rattlesnakes and six-shooters. Not so far from wrong there, actually.

The only reason Felicia was in Albuquerque, of course, was me. I got the distinct impression it would be fine with her, and with her parents, if she'd made such a choice for a man with a future. But I was more like a man with a past. Not the kind of guy a woman enjoys showing off for her family.

My food went sour in my mouth. I put down my fork.

It wasn't so much that her parents were coming. I could put on the dog for them for a couple of days: make my career sound better than it was, mind my manners, maybe even buy a necktie. It was more the notion that Felicia might be ashamed of me.

Sure, I'm not exactly a prime catch, more like a little fish you'd throw back. No money, no prospects, less hair all the time. But I'm man enough to keep her happy most of the time. Shouldn't that be enough for her parents? For her?

"What's the matter?" She'd caught my sudden change in mood.

"Nothing."

"Oh, don't take it so hard. It won't be that bad if they come." She was misreading me, thinking I was just nervous about meeting her parents. I let her think so.

"When are they coming?"

"It's not firm yet. Probably in a month or two."

"Good. That gives me time to become rich and successful before we meet."

"Hardly. And I don't care about that, anyway."

Her tone said she did care, at least a little.

"Well, at least it's long enough for this shiner to disappear."

"That would be nice."

T H R E E
■ ◆ ■

The telephone jolted me awake the next morning. I'd eased my depression by finishing off the bourbon the night before, and the bell set off trip-hammers inside my head.

"Hullo?"

"Bubba Mabry? This is Marcus Ogletroop."

Ogletroop? Why did that name sound familiar?

"I want to talk to you about a possible job. That is, my grandmother wants to see you. How soon could you come to our house?"

I told him I could be there in an hour, and he gave me an address near the Albuquerque Country Club. Then he hung up. Quick, businesslike.

I cradled the phone, fell back onto my pillow, and had almost drifted back off to sleep when I remembered where I'd heard that name. Ogletroop. The Goddess.

I leaped out of bed, ignoring the pounding of my hangover, and went straight to the shower. If the Ogletroops wanted to send some of their considerable riches my way, I shouldn't keep them

18

waiting. This could be an opportunity to pull out of my financial slump. And wouldn't Felicia be impressed!

The Ogletroop house overlooked the golf course. *House* isn't a strong-enough word. Mansion, at least. Palace, maybe. It was a rambling two-story affair with stucco walls, a Spanish tile roof, and wrought-iron balconies. Giant cottonwoods threw long, ragged inkblots of shade across the wide lawn. I parked around the corner, on a side street, and made my way across the lawn to the front door. Better that the Ogletroops not see my car in their driveway. I didn't want to do anything that might lower their opinion of me, assuming they had an opinion. Maybe they were having every private eye in town trot through their house until they found the right one. I was determined that would be me, even if they'd called me last.

I pushed a button by the front door, setting off melodious chimes inside. I studied my reflection in the window, straightening my hair, flashing a quick smile to make sure nothing was stuck to my front teeth. I'd put on my navy blue sport coat for the occasion, had my white shirt buttoned all the way up. I looked pretty respectable for a guy with a shiner.

A stout Hispanic woman in a black-and-white maid's uniform answered the door. I told her my name, and she gestured me inside. The foyer was bigger than my entire home at the Desert Breeze, with shiny white tile and an antique armoire. A curving staircase swept up to a balcony, enclosed by more wrought-iron railings. The maid had gone off to fetch her boss, and he arrived before I could look around more.

Marcus Ogletroop looked like he spent a lot of time on tennis courts: sun-lightened hair, a nice tan, a spring in his step. He was my age or a little younger—mid-thirties—but he looked younger, healthier, more virile. He had a dimpled jaw like Kirk Douglas and shoulders like a linebacker. He didn't look particularly happy to see me, but he crunched my hand in welcome.

"My grandmother is ill," he said. "Follow me, and I'll take you to her room."

I trooped off down the hallway behind him, trying to put a price tag on his double-breasted gray suit, which had a soft drape that had Italian design written all over it. He wore shiny loafers with little tassels on them. I wouldn't be caught dead in shoes like that, which is fine, because I could never afford them, anyway.

Most of the rooms along the wide corridor were closed off by sliding wooden doors, but I got glimpses into a few that were open. Persian rugs, overstuffed furniture, paintings in gilt frames. Lush, lush, lush. It was as if I was on a movie set decorated to convey wealth. My reality meter sprung its works.

They had me. The advantage of self-employment is being able to walk away from distasteful jobs. But I was so overwhelmed by my surroundings, the Ogletroops could've proposed anything and I would've taken it. Assassination, train robbery, septic-tank diving. Yes, sir, break out the brandy and cigars. I'm your man.

Marcus knocked on a door, heard some signal from beyond, and opened it. We stepped into Mrs. Ogletroop's bedroom, the Goddess's inner sanctum. The walls were paneled in dark wood, but French doors spilled light into the room and allowed a view of a rose garden beyond.

Mrs. Ogletroop sat up very straight in her four-poster bed, propped up by satin-covered pillows. She must've been at least eighty, but I could see at a glance that she'd once been a beauty, tall and regal, with a neck as long and graceful as Nefertiti's. Her white hair was swept up and pinned back, and she wore a full complement of makeup and a pink silk peignoir. A file of computer spreadsheets was open in her lap, and she closed it and set it aside with arthritis-gnarled hands.

"Leave us, Penny," she said. "We need to talk."

A white-uniformed nurse whom I hadn't even noticed rose

silently from a chair in the corner and slipped out of the room, closing the door behind her.

"Have a seat, Mr. Mabry."

"Call me Bubba." I took the chair the nurse had vacated. Marcus hung back by the door, his hands in his pockets, his eyes on his grandmother.

"What happened to your eye?"

Marcus hadn't said anything about my shiner, and I'd been so caught up in studying the mansion that I'd forgotten all about it.

"I, uh, walked into a door."

Mrs. Ogletroop gave me a demure smile. "How careless of you."

"Accidents happen when you least expect them. If I'd known I'd be coming to see you, I would've made sure to watch where I was going."

She smiled again. This was encouraging.

"We were referred to you by our city councilwoman and dear friend, Alice Burden. She said you had helped her in the past, and you're very discreet."

Alice, sweet Alice. I'd recovered a doll collection that had been stolen from her, and she'd remembered. I owed her now. Big time.

"Since I've taken ill," she said, "I don't have the strength or, frankly, the patience for long conversations. We'd like to hire you for a matter involving my granddaughter. It must be confidential."

"Yes, ma'am."

"I'll let Marcus fill you in on the details."

Marcus stepped forward and cleared his throat, ready to do his part.

"My sister, Margaret, has fallen in with some very strange people. We want to get her away from them."

I nodded.

"Near Taos, there's an old ranch that's been taken over by a group of women. They call themselves Women Overcoming the Masculine Burden, or WOMB.

"Margaret's had some bad experiences with men over the past few years, some broken romances, and I think that's what led her up there. The idea of being surrounded by other women, women who understand her, lured her into WOMB, and now we can't get her out. I've gone up there a few times; we've telephoned. They won't even let us talk to her. Frankly, Mr. Mabry, we're worried. This WOMB seems like a cult to me. We've heard some pretty weird stories about what goes on there."

I shifted in my chair. "Like what?"

"Pagan sacrifices, animal mutilations, witchcraft. Maybe it's a lot of tripe, but we don't know what to believe at this point."

Mrs. Ogletroop seemed to be resting while Marcus spoke. Her eyelids drooped and she leaned more heavily against her pillows.

"We've hired a man who specializes in this sort of thing," Marcus continued. "A cult deprogrammer. His name is Purvis Reasons, and he comes highly recommended. He's already up in Taos, ready to get Margaret out, but he needs somebody to help him, to watch his back. We don't want any slipups. We don't want Margaret hurt any more than she already has been."

I sat forward, rested my elbows on my knees.

"How long has Margaret been up there?"

"Nine months."

"And you haven't seen her in all that time?"

"Not once. She never leaves WOMB. She's written us a few letters, assuring us everything is fine. But how can we believe that when they won't let her leave?"

"If they're holding her against her will, it's kidnapping."

"She swears that's not the case. Her letters say she's happy there. For the first time in her life, she's happy."

Mrs. Ogletroop stirred at that, opened her eyes.

"If it's a cult," she said, "if they've brainwashed her, she would say anything. Margaret was always a happy child, high-spirited, carefree. Her parents, Marcus's parents, were killed in a car wreck when the children were young. I raised them myself, and they never wanted for anything."

Marcus nodded through this explanation.

"That's what has us so mystified," he said quickly. "Her letters make it sound like she was miserable until she hooked up with WOMB. We know that just wasn't the case."

An awkward silence filled the room.

"So," I said finally, "you want me and this deprogrammer, Reasons, to snatch her?"

Marcus winced at my blunt words.

"We want her safe," he said. "If that means spiriting her away from that place, then fine, do it. If you can't do that, then at least talk to her, make sure they haven't done something terrible to her."

Mrs. Ogletroop studied me.

"We want someone to watch Mr. Reasons," she said. "Not that we don't trust him, but he's a strange little man, very devout, very intense. He seems like the kind of man who takes chances, and we can't have that. This must all be very low-key, very quiet."

I nodded to show I understood.

"We're willing to pay you very well to take on this job," she said. "Marcus."

Marcus reached inside his jacket and pulled out a fat creamy envelope. He handed it to me.

"There's a thousand dollars in there," he said. "That should cover your expenses and act as a retainer. Keep a careful accounting of your hours and expenses."

My hand shook as I took the envelope.

"How soon can you leave?" he asked.

"I can be in Taos this afternoon."

"Fine. Stay at the Holiday Inn. I'll call Reasons and have him get in touch with you. He's been studying WOMB, and he can fill you in on the details."

I rose from the chair, felt like I could float right up to the ceiling. A thousand dollars. I'd snatch Mu'ammar Gadhafi out of his Bedouin tent for that much money.

"Thank you, Mr. Mabry," Mrs. Ogletroop said. "I think you're going to be a great help to us."

"Yes, ma'am, I'll do my best."

I followed Marcus into the hallway. The nurse had been waiting in the hall, and he let her back inside the bedroom before he softly closed the door.

As we walked back toward the front of the house, I said, "Is your grandmother real sick?"

"She's dying, I'm afraid. Her heart's simply worn out. And it doesn't help that Margaret is breaking it by running off like this."

Just inside the front door, he paused, turned toward me.

"Margaret and I stand to inherit a great deal when my grandmother passes on," he said, just above a whisper, as if the Goddess could hear everything in her grand old house. "I'm afraid Margaret will give away her share, turn it over to WOMB. That would complicate matters."

I could see that. Imagine if the *Albuquerque Gazette* suddenly was half-owned by a feminist cult. That could scare off a lot of advertisers, not to mention subscribers. People don't like you to monkey around with their morning newspaper. Something as simple as dropping a comic strip is enough to get every cranky retiree in the state writing in to complain.

"I'll be in touch," he said. "If you need anything, call me."

He handed me a business card printed with only his name and a trio of phone numbers. Then he somberly shook my hand and showed me to the door.

24

I practically skipped across the Ogletroops' lawn. Once I was safely in my car, I opened the envelope and counted the money. Twenty crisp fifty-dollar bills. I cackled like a crazy person. It had been a long time since I'd had this much money at once.

I cranked the starter, and the Chevy, recognizing my good mood, immediately roared to life. I drove away, watching for a pay phone. I had to call Felicia.

F O U R
■ ◆ ■

"City Desk. Quattlebaum."

It sounded as if the phone had been answered by a barking dog. Felicia was in a bad mood—again.

"Hi, babe, it's me. How about some lunch?"

"I don't know, Bubba, I'm really busy. . . ."

"I just landed a job. I've got a pocketful of money. And I need to pick your brain."

"My brain?"

"You know anything about a place called WOMB?"

"Some kind of commune, isn't it? Up near Taos?"

"That's the one. I'm headed up there this afternoon, and I need to get some information before I go."

"I guess I could see if we have anything in the library here. But it's going to be hard to get away."

"It's a very important client. Name of Ogletroop."

"Ogletroop? Marcus hired you?"

"Well, he was there. But it was really Mrs. Ogletroop who hired me. She thinks I'm the right man for the job."

"The Goddess? You met her? In person?"

"Yup."

"How soon do you want to meet?"

We agreed to lunch at Fat Jack's; a saloon near the newspaper office, it features sports and country-music videos on giant TV screens. A nice noisy place where we wouldn't have to worry about being overheard. And they make some of the biggest hamburgers in the world.

I stopped by my place and threw some clothes and my revolver into a gym bag. I stashed four of the fifty-dollar bills and Kathy Grabow's check under the drawer in my nightstand. Even if things went wrong in Taos, I'd have that money to fall back on when I got home.

I was ordering my second beer by the time Felicia came blowing through the door of Fat Jack's. She ordered a Coke and waited for the waitress to move away before she pulled a sheaf of Xerox copies out of her purse.

"Here's everything we have on WOMB," she said. "There's less there than meets the eye. They're a very secretive bunch. One of the state-desk reporters has been trying to do a feature on them for about a year, but they won't play along."

I glanced at the clippings, then folded them and stuck them in my hip pocket. Plenty of time for that later. For now, I wanted to bask in Felicia's undivided attention.

"So tell me about the Goddess," she said. "What does she look like?"

"You've never seen her?"

"She doesn't come to the office. Runs everything from that big house of hers. Marcus is the only one who ever comes around, poking into the business. Acts like he's running the show, but everybody knows it's the Goddess who pulls the strings."

"I imagine that's the case. She seems like a very assertive woman."

I ran it all down for her: the mansion, the mission, the Goddess propped up in bed like a dowager empress. Margaret Ogletroop's disappearance into WOMB was news to Felicia, as was the Goddess's heart condition.

"The family keeps its distance from the newspaper," she explained. "That's really for the best. They've got a lot of business interests that could conflict, but we don't even know what they are. Occasionally, Marcus will come down to the newsroom, have a closed-door meeting with the editor, and some project will disappear. But we're never told why."

"That must make you a little crazy."

"Well, it keeps us speculating. Just like this story I've been working on. The paper supported the governor when he ran for reelection, so I have to assume he's friends with the Goddess. But I don't know if the pressure to drop the story comes from her, or from Marcus, or if my editors are just as idiotic as they seem."

Our burgers arrived, and we wolfed them.

"What about Margaret Ogletroop?" I asked her through a mouthful. "You know anything about her?"

Felicia swallowed, said, "Debutante. Went to Vassar. Hasn't done much since she got back to Albuquerque, except go to country club parties and snort cocaine."

"Really? A drug problem?"

"I don't know how much of a problem it is. Or was. It was all just scuttlebutt. And if she's gone to WOMB, that's all in the past. I don't think they do drugs up there. They're all high on anger."

"What are they so angry about? Men?"

Felicia nodded, a twinkle in her eye.

"What did we do to make them mad?"

"You'd have to be a woman to understand it."

"A lot of stuff seems to fall into that category. I thought things were changing, what with feminism and all. Women don't seem so oppressed to me anymore."

Felicia leaned back in her seat, sizing me up. I never know when to stop talking.

"Look at you," I said. "Nice career. Good income. Lots of choices about your life. What's so terrible?"

Felicia shook her head at my stupidity, but she was smiling.

"Look, Bubba, some things men just can't understand. Even a pillar of southern enlightenment such as yourself."

She likes to take those little shots at me, at the fact that I'm from Mississippi, like I haven't outgrown my redneck roots.

"Until you've walked a mile in my high heels . . ." She shrugged, let the rest go unsaid.

"Okay, if you don't want to discuss sociology with me, I'd better get going. I've got a long drive ahead."

I paid the waitress, watching Felicia to see if her eyebrows shot up at the sight of me with a fifty-dollar bill. But she was staring at some hunk on one of the big-screen TVs and didn't even notice.

Outside, I thanked her for her help, gave her a peck on the cheek, and told her I'd see her in a few days.

As I hit the road, I was grinning like a mule eating sawbriars. A full belly, a wallet full of money, a full tank of gas, and a job to do. Who could ask for anything more? A little more appreciation from my beloved would've been nice, but, hey, you can't have everything. Felicia was impressed that I'd met the Goddess, and that was worth something. That Mrs. Ogletroop had seen fit to hire me had to raise me in Felicia's estimation, even if she wouldn't come right out and say it.

You want to be admired by those who love you. Otherwise, their love is a gift, a bonus you didn't earn. Call it primitive if you like, but men feel as if they have to be the breadwinners, the hunters, and they want to be admired for those efforts. It's not enough to slay the deer and take it back to the campfire. They want to tell the story of the hunt again and again, and they want the rapt attention of the women while they tell it.

True, I'm far from being Felicia's breadwinner. We don't even share the same roof, and she makes much more money than I do, delivered in regular weekly paychecks. I barely survive from one slain deer to the next. But I still find myself doing things in search of her praise, more so than I'd ever admit to her.

Felicia doesn't recognize this. Being the cynical reporter she is, she's much quicker to point out my failures than my successes. The failures are more common and easier to see. My every short-coming is more ammunition for her arguments that I should give up being a private eye and get some regular job, sitting at a desk, gathering stability like so much moss. No wonder I try to make each case sound like a job for Superman.

I know I'm something of a stumblebum, that the gullibility that runs in my family means I'll never give Philip Marlowe a run for his money as a great detective. But I don't want *her* to see that.

Men want to be heroes. Look at little Marty Grabow. A fail-ure in front of his woman and he went limp. Stand somebody like me in front of him, let him take a few pokes at me, and he's virile again, ready to ride off and fight the dragons for his lady love.

Fortunately, men are blessed with short memories. No mat-ter how many failures we stack up, the next victory is just around the corner. And even the slightest success is enough to get us puffed up and thumping our chests again.

Just getting hired by the Ogletroops when I had so much going against me (not the least of which was the shiner I kept checking in the rearview mirror) seemed enough like a success to keep me grinning all the way to Taos.

F I V E

■◆■

I hadn't been to Taos in years, and I'd forgotten just how gorgeous a drive it is. The sixty miles to Santa Fe were pretty much a big empty—rolling desert, with only the distant mountains to keep my eyes busy. But once I was through the crowded streets of the capital, the highway unfolded as one picture postcard after another.

The sky was doing its best impression of Indian jewelry, turquoise blue glinting with silvery sunlight. And the land alternated between arid yellow and the deep green of the river valleys. The highway wound through steep-sided canyons alongside the Rio Grande for much of the trip, so steep that the state had erected chain-link fences to catch falling rocks before they could crush the cars below. The fences bulged with their loads of stone, making me uneasy. Naturally, they'd put up no fence along the cliffs that lined the river side of the road, not even a barrier to keep cars from flying off into space. Didn't want to mess up the view of the river, I guess. Here and there, I spotted orange rubber rafts full of tourists braving the white water below.

Not long after I passed into Taos County, the highway switch-backed up out of a canyon and onto the high, sagebrush-furred plain that stretched all the way to Wheeler Peak and the other mountains that loomed over the town. From the road, I could see in the distance the Rio Grande Gorge, a deep slash carved into black volcanic rock by the river. Tourists in Winnebagos were pulled off at picnic areas on either side of the road, soaking in the views and baking in the sun. I drove on, a man on a mission.

The highway rippled through little villages and tourist traps the last few miles before it entered Taos, then suddenly became a wide four-lane lined with convenience stores and ski shops and real estate offices. Taos had grown from sleepy Indian village to trendy artist colony to adobe Disneyland over the past few generations, and the commercial strip spread ever southward.

The Holiday Inn was along that stretch of road, but I treated myself to a quick drive through town before circling back to the motel that would be my base of operations. A sign at the city limits said Taos had an elevation of 6,967 feet. No indication of the population, though I figured it to be somewhere around six thousand. New Mexico towns don't display the population, because then they'd have to keep updating the signs. You can trust elevation to remain steady.

The road narrowed again as it climbed a hill to the crumbling adobe buildings around the plaza. This was the old Taos, the picturesque mercantile establishments and houses and trading posts. Now, the buildings held T-shirt shops and chic bistros and endless art galleries. Orange poppies and towering hollyhocks danced in their beds alongside the street, bouncing in the breeze from passing cars. The sidewalks teemed with equally colorful tourists in the bright plumage of determined recreation—plaid shorts over pale, skinny legs, lemon golf shirts, paisley sundresses, neon bicycle spandex, hats of every description. I spotted a few apparent New Agers, garbed in beads and feathers, come to Taos for the healing auras.

Taos is reputed to be a magical place, bathed in the crisp sunlight you find at high altitudes. The mountains rise up behind it like big-shouldered gods, making you feel small and blessed at the same time. The place is a magnet for New Agers, who seek the wisdom of the ancients and the power of nature. I recalled that several years ago Taos was proclaimed one of the main "power points" by the wackos who participated in a worldwide gathering called Harmonic Convergence. Those folks believed that if they met at the globe's power points, held hands and chanted, they could change the world, could bring about peace. Since then, the Cold War thawed out, the Berlin Wall came down, and the nuclear clock ran backward, relieving us all of the burden of potential holocaust. Hmm. Maybe they were onto something.

Lost in such thoughts, I chugged along behind a low-rider Buick with throbbing exhaust pipes, doing the requisite eight miles per hour. Taos, like a lot of the New Mexican tourist towns, had essentially been stolen away from the Indians and Hispanics, who were there first, and it seemed that the only way they could still throw their weight around was in traffic. They might've been priced out of the real estate market, relegated to some dilapidated mobile home on the outskirts of town, but they could still afford a big, loud car to thunder at the tourists.

I turned onto Garcia Street to get out from behind the low-rider, got momentarily lost in a maze of backstreets, then circled around the plaza and headed back south.

The Holiday Inn, like most everything else in Taos, was done up in a flat-roofed, brown stucco style intended to approximate adobe. I'd passed the real deal—the old Sagebrush Inn—on the way into town, and would've preferred to stay there, since somebody else was paying. But Marcus Ogletroop had said Reasons would hunt me down at the Holiday Inn, and that's where I'd be.

The desk clerk wore a buttoned green vest that made him look like a leprechaun, along with a hangdog expression that made him look weary. After three hours on the road, I was pretty eager to get to a bathroom, but the clerk was not to be hurried as he thumbed through reservation cards and located my key. I swapped him some cash for the key, then asked, "Any messages for me?"

The clerk sighed and rolled his eyes, then turned back to his pigeonholes to fumble around for messages. He finally came up with one, handed it over, and told me how to find my room. The motel was arranged in pueblolike clumps of rooms, each named after some Taos luminary like Kit Carson or D. H. Lawrence. I was assigned to a room in the Georgia O'Keeffe wing, way around on the backside of the complex.

I waited until I was outside to read my message, which was penned in neat, rounded script. It said: "Meet me for dinner at 7:00 P.M. at the Plaza Café. I'll wait for you out front. Purvis Reasons."

I had a couple of hours. After enjoying a long-awaited pee in the sparkling bathroom of my room, I unpacked, opened the drapes to a view of the mountains to the east, and settled down in an armchair with the clippings Felicia had given me.

It didn't take long to see she was right. There wasn't much to the newspaper stories. The WOMBsters had jealously guarded their privacy, deflecting the natural interest in an all-female commune. I did learn the ranch was northeast of Taos proper, in the high-priced land between the town and the ski resort, and that it belonged to a Vivian Bankhead, who'd inherited it from her father, a painter who'd been one of the founders of the Taos artists' colony back in the 1930s. There'd been some dispute among the Bankhead family when Vivian invited all her female friends to move onto the ranch and set up housekeeping, but after one court appearance, the whole thing had been hushed up.

The other clippings concerned a neighboring rancher who'd tried to blame the women at WOMB for a couple of cattle mutilations that had happened on his land. The rancher, Jeronimo Valdez, a fifth-generation Taoseño, had told the reporter he often heard strange drumming music floating over from WOMB, and he suspected witchcraft went on over there. It seemed natural enough, to him, to blame witches for the deaths of his cows, which had had their udders, eyes, and other unnamed parts removed with "surgical precision."

Cattle mutilations were nothing new in New Mexico. A couple of times a year, the newspapers fill up with reports that someone or something is dismembering cows with "surgical precision." I knew from past reading that most were dismissed by law-enforcement officials as being the work of posthumous bloat and skilled buzzards with razor-sharp beaks. But like anything people don't understand, it's more fun to blame witches or scalpel-waving Satanists or UFOs.

Anyhow, all the newspaper reporter had been able to get out of many phone calls to WOMB was a terse "No comment." If they were mutilating cattle, they weren't saying.

I still had some time. I fought off the urge to take a nap, figuring I'd oversleep. I wanted to make a good impression on Purvis Reasons. I wasn't accustomed to working with anyone else on a case—though sometimes Felicia succeeds in butting in—and the prospect made me anxious. It didn't help that the Ogletroops wanted me keeping an eye on him, preventing him from doing anything rash. I'm such a plodder that rashness tends to catch me off guard.

All I needed to remind me of that was a look in the mirror.

The shiner had darkened somewhat, more of a royal purple than a lavender, but it clearly would be with me for days, maybe a week.

I washed up, bought a seventy-five-cent Coke out of a glowing machine around the corner, and flipped through cable TV channels until it was time to go.

The sun was low in the west and the streets had emptied out, though the patios in front of a couple of cafés still were packed with diners. I lucked into a parking space right on the plaza and arrived in front of the Plaza Café, which was tucked away down an alley, at exactly seven o'clock.

"Bubba Mabry?"

A man stepped from the shadows alongside the café.

"That's me. You must be Mr. Reasons."

He was a small man, and his bony hand disappeared in mine when we shook. He was dressed all in black, which always makes me think of Johnny Cash, and devoid of ornamentation except for a single piece of jewelry, a three-inch-long silver cross that hung on a chain around his neck. He looked like a priest or an ascetic monk, pale and thin. His graying brown hair was cut short around small, pointy ears, but a forelock drooped down nearly to his eyebrows. He had narrow pale green eyes that I could feel sweeping over me.

"What happened to your eye?"

"I got struck by lightning."

He pursed his thin lips at such an obvious lie, then shrugged and jerked his head toward the restaurant door. People frankly stared at the two of us as we waited to be seated. I try so hard to blend into the crowd, to disappear into the woodwork, and here I was with someone who looked like he should be in a stained-glass window.

Reasons waited until an effeminate waiter had seated us in a corner before he spoke again.

"How much did the Ogletroops tell you about our mission?" His voice was just above a whisper, and his lips didn't seem to move. For a second, I wasn't sure he had spoken at all. It was as if his words had just appeared in my mind. A scary thought.

"Just the basics," I said, trying to use the same low tone. "Young Margaret disappeared into WOMB nine months ago, and they haven't seen her since."

"Did they tell you much about WOMB?"

"They didn't seem to know much. I was hoping you'd scouted it out."

"I haven't been up there yet. The Ogletroops told me to wait until I had some muscle backing me up."

His eyes roamed over me again, sizing me up, and I could tell from the cloud that crossed his face that I was much less muscle than he had expected.

"Frankly, Mr. Mabry, I would've preferred to bring in my own people. There are dozens of experienced people around the country I could've summoned for such a job, people who've worked with cults before. I'm assuming that you haven't?"

Something about the way he flattened his *r*'s said *Yankee* to my southern-born ears. Growing up, I was always taught never to trust a Yankee. Folks in Mississippi are still mad about the War Between the States and the carpetbaggers who followed that humbling defeat. I've tried to overcome this prejudice—Albuquerque abounds in transplanted New Yorkers who are potential clients—but I haven't been totally successful. Any hint of Yankee in somebody's voice and my hand goes protectively to my wallet.

"No, I've never investigated a cult before."

Reasons shook his head and sighed. I get that reaction a lot.

"I guess it doesn't really matter," he said. "WOMB seems to be a one-of-a-kind operation, anyway. We'll be breaking new ground here."

"How's that?"

"From what I've been able to learn, WOMB is based on worshiping the goddess. Do you know about the goddess?"

For an instant, I thought he meant the WOMBsters worshiped Mrs. Ogletroop. But I caught myself, and merely shook my head.

"A lot of pagan groups around the country are trying to get back to the old ways that existed before Christianity. Most of the religions back then believed the Earth was a woman, or was created by a woman, and they worshiped her."

My eyes dropped to the cross around Reasons's neck, but I forced them back to his face. He didn't seem to notice my distraction.

"A lot of the goddess worshipers who exist today also dabble in witchcraft and astrology and New Age stuff. You've heard about some of that?"

"Oh, sure. It's everywhere you look. I saw a bumper sticker today that said, 'Life is a witch and then you fly.' "

He nodded, his lips pursed, as if he wanted me to shut up so he could continue. I obliged, but our waiter swished up to the table about then and we had to order. I'd scarcely glanced at the menu, though I had spotted escargot and squid among the appetizers. Playing it safe, I ordered enchiladas. Reasons ordered a big salad, dressing on the side.

"All right," he said after the waiter moved away, "it's pretty clear that, since they're named Women Overcoming the Masculine Burden, infiltration by either of us is out. That's pretty risky with any kind of cult, anyway."

"Why's that?"

"With a lot of cults, you go in, and you never come out."

"They kill people?"

Reasons smiled for the first time—prim, no teeth showing.

"If they have to. But that's not their usual tactic. It's all about mind control, Mr. Mabry. Even the strongest of minds is vulnerable."

I didn't like the way he was looking at me. Like my mind wasn't one of the strongest.

"They don't let you sleep. They talk to you constantly. They teach you to chant and meditate away all your doubts. They teach you that you're special, that you've been chosen by God to join them, and pretty soon you believe it."

I shook my head. After growing up among Bible-thumping Baptists in Mississippi, I felt impervious to religion. If you can shake off that upbringing, you can do anything. It was particularly strong in my own household, where my mother, Eloise Cutwaller Mabry, believed she had visitations from Jesus. Try growing up in a small town where everybody knows your mother likes to chat with the Lord while feeding him peach cobbler in her own kitchen. Hell, Mama was written up in national newspapers by reporters whose chortling you could practically hear in their prose. Her faith was unshaken. Mine never recovered.

"Believe it, Mr. Mabry," Reasons said. "I've seen it plenty of times. There are hundreds, maybe thousands, of these groups around the country, preying on people who are at some weak point in their lives—divorces, unemployment, deaths in their families."

"Marcus Ogletroop said Margaret had some busted romances."

"Exactly. She's turned off on men, been treated badly, and along come some women who say, 'We don't need men. We're special. The goddess loves us.' "

The food arrived. I wolfed the enchiladas, which were made of nutty blue corn and hot, hot green chile. Reasons picked at his salad. I noticed he didn't put any salad dressing on it. I'd just as soon eat hay as plain lettuce, but he didn't seem to mind.

Between bites, I asked him how deprogramming works.

"First, you have to isolate the person from the other cult members. Catch them off the grounds, or snatch them. Then, you go to work on them, trying to reprogram the brainwashing they've undergone."

"How do you do that?"

"It's not easy. The techniques are much the same as the cults use. You talk to them constantly, keep them awake, show them videotapes about the dangers of mind control. Eventually, they break. They start to see how their lives have been taken over by the cult, how God doesn't necessarily want zealots."

"Or, in this case, the goddess."

"Yes, I suppose that's right, though I'm going to have a hard time telling Margaret anything about the goddess with a straight face. I believe in the biblical God. It might be tough, though, to steer her from one whole belief system to another. We'll have to see whether that's possible, or if we have to appeal to the pagan beliefs WOMB has instilled in her."

I didn't like the sound of that. Let the woman believe whatever she wants. Just get her back to her family, and let the psychiatrists sort out the rest. Reasons's cheeks were flushed with the thrill of a possible conversion. No wonder the Ogletroops wanted him watched.

He seemed to recognize he'd said too much, and he went back to munching his salad. I finally broke the silence by saying, "How'd you get involved in this line of work?"

He set down his fork.

"I was caught up in a cult myself. In Idaho. I'd come out west to find myself, and somebody else found me first."

"How long were you trapped in there?"

"Trapped? I wouldn't say trapped. At the time, it was the only place I ever wanted to be. We seemed like right-thinking people, all living good lives, all united in our vision of the Lord. It was only when the leader of the cult started 'marrying' one female member after another that I realized something had gone wrong. Fortunately for me, my parents had never given up trying to get me out. A deprogrammer from Chicago kidnapped me, took me to a cabin out in the mountains, and worked with me for a week before I started to come around."

"A week?"

"I was a hard case. They'd controlled me completely. See what I mean, Mr. Mabry? We're all vulnerable."

"So that's when you became a deprogrammer yourself?"

"No, it took several years of counseling just to get myself back together. Only after that was complete did I realize I'd been called by the Lord to do this work."

My skin crawled. Anytime someone claims to have been singled out by God, I immediately assume insanity. I always figured that God, if He exists at all, is too busy to point His big finger at individuals. Just keeping all the planets in their orbits was a job not unlike the guy on the old *Ed Sullivan Show* who spun plates on long, flexible sticks. Keeping all those plates spinning was enough to keep any deity busy. Much too busy to be scanning a roll of 6 billion people, picking which ones would do his work.

Reasons smiled, which didn't make me feel any better.

"And now, Mr. Mabry, you've been called, as well."

S I X
■ ◆ ■

My idea of the great outdoors is tooling along the Cruise with
the windows rolled down. New Mexico is crawling with out-
doorsmen—hikers and hunters, campers and climbers—but I'm
not one of them. I prefer asphalt and concrete to forests and
mountains. In the city, you don't have to worry about snakes—
the legless variety, anyway—or bears or mountain lions or any
other dangers of the wild. I got enough of that growing up in the
piney woods of Mississippi, where snakes will slither right into
your house without even bothering to knock.

Yet here I was, tiptoeing through the underbrush down a
steep slope, ducking tree branches and ready to run like hell at
the first sign of a rattlesnake. Purvis Reasons moved ahead of me,
scouting the forest, making scarcely a sound. It seemed as if I
stepped on every dry twig he missed, slipped on every rock he
stealthily avoided. I probably sounded like an elephant herd moving through the trees. Though it was still chilly, I was sweating
like a sinner in church.

We'd met as planned at dawn Friday and had taken Reasons's rental car out of town, northwest on Highway 64. We'd turned when we reached state highway 150, the road that leads to Taos Ski Valley. When that narrow two-lane reached Arroyo Seco, a little burg whose old buildings squeezed tightly to the shoulders of the road, Reasons had turned off on a gravel road that bumped over hills, headed toward the cloud-capped peaks. Weeds and wildflowers grew tall alongside the road, and old elms and cottonwoods leaned their shade over us.

The entrance to WOMB was just a dirt track disappearing into the trees. A rusty steel cable was strung across the driveway, from which hung a sign that read succinctly, KEEP OUT.

Reasons had pointed out the entrance, then had driven on past, swinging up onto an even bumpier side road that climbed toward a spruce-dotted ridge. He'd told me the road dead-ended at Jeronimo Valdez's small ranch, which was why no houses or barns interrupted the lush landscape of trees and flowering bushes. The fences on the right side of the road belonged to Valdez. They were old and rusty and the rough posts leaned. On the left, a shiny mesh fence stretched tight as a girdle around WOMB. Reasons had found a wide spot on the shoulder to park, and we'd climbed over the fence and plunged into the thick woods.

It was slow going. Valdez's land appeared to roll away toward the mountains, but the slope on the WOMB side of the road dropped nearly straight down. We struggled along, trying to be quiet, holding on to trees to keep from tumbling. When we were nearly to the bottom, Reasons spotted sunlight glinting off a window, and we realized we were close. We circled the settlement, creeping along, keeping low, trying to find a vantage point.

The trees opened where a giant old pine had toppled and taken out its neighbors. The decomposing log was covered with terraces of orange fungus and looked as if it harbored snakes and bugs and other vermin, but Reasons crouched down behind it and I joined him.

An old adobe ranch house and several newer buildings filled the clearing below. A creek rippled through the far edge of the clearing, and near it were two honest-to-God tepees, standing tall like sentinels from the past, decorated with red paint in the shapes of frolicking women and stylized animals.

Reasons had brought a set of binoculars in a belt pack, and he used them now to focus on the buildings. I had to be content with squinting.

Trees and thick underbrush surrounded the clearing, except for where the dirt driveway plunged away on the opposite side over a rickety-looking bridge. As we watched, a woman ducked out the door of one of the tepees and made her way across the clearing to a small building that I guessed was the outhouse. Bigger and nicer than any outhouse I'd ever seen back in Mississippi, but where else did one go first thing in the morning?

We watched WOMB for an hour as the place came to life. Women, many dressed in what appeared to be buckskin, strolled from one building to another, some holding hands like schoolgirls. Smoke trailed from a chimney at the main house. All was peaceful and quiet.

I felt like an Indian spying on a pioneer settlement a hundred years ago. Granted, a clumsy Indian, in a blue shirt that probably stood out from the surrounding woods like a flag. Reasons was better prepared, dressed in a tan camouflage shirt and black pants. He also wore hiking boots with treaded soles, as opposed to my old slick sneakers, and I took some comfort in that, attributing his natural stealthiness to classier footwear.

When Reasons paused from his binoculars to rub his eyes, I whispered, "Have you spotted her?"

Reasons had a photograph of Margaret in his car, a studio shot provided by the family, and we'd both studied it before leaving the car parked along the road. The photo showed a young woman with long blond hair and perfect teeth. She looked a lot like her brother, but without the tan, and she wore a strapless gown that showed off creamy shoulders.

Reasons shook his head at my question. If Margaret was down below in WOMB, she wasn't out and about this morning.

"Of course," he whispered after a moment, "if she's been here nine months, she could look appreciably different from that photo. Most of the women I've seen have their hair cut short, and they're wearing feathers and beads and moccasins. Maybe I looked right at her and didn't realize it."

I itched for a turn at the binoculars, but Reasons put them back to his eyes and intently studied the scene some more. I leaned back on my elbows, no longer worrying about centipedes or spiders. Waiting and watching are the toughest parts of my job, and it didn't help that I couldn't see much from where we perched.

Something skittered in the leaves behind us, and that got me sitting up and turning around. Just in time to see two amazons plunge through the trees and set upon us.

I had my gun on my hip, but it all happened so fast, I didn't even think to try for it. Reasons didn't even have time to take the binoculars from his eyes.

They were tall women, one willowy as a model and the other butch and burly as a stevedore. The thin one had a wicked-looking hunting bow with an arrow strung up and ready to fire; the other carried a spear with a flint point like something out of a museum. The thin one planted a moccasin in the middle of Reasons's back and aimed the razorlike arrowhead at his scalp. The spear point stopped just shy of my nose.

The big woman hissed at me, "Freeze!"

I raised my hands and said, "Frozen."

The willowy woman tossed back her long brown hair and said

calmly to the back of Reason's head, "You're trespassing."

The other one said, "And this one's got a gun."

She grabbed one of my upraised arms by the wrist and flipped me over as deftly as a wrestler. My face cracked against the log, and I got a mouthful of fungus. My black eye sent a throb through the rest of my head. I felt her yank my revolver from its holster.

I turned back toward her, spitting and hacking. She'd stuck my gun in her belt and had the spear pointed at me.

Reasons still sprawled across the log, the binoculars limp in his hand. Without turning, he said, "We mean no harm. We're here to talk to someone."

"Don't look to me like you're talking," said the burly woman. "Looks like you're Peeping Toms. Fuckin' men."

The other one took her foot off Reasons, took a step backward.

"Now, Judah," she said, "no sense in getting ugly with them. We'll take them to Luna and let her decide what to do."

Judah, the linebacker, looked like she wanted to say more, or maybe just skewer me, but after an internal struggle, she clamped her mouth shut and nodded brusquely.

"On your feet."

Reasons and I clambered upright, keeping our hands plainly visible and moving slowly. I glanced over at him, and he didn't look the least bit scared. Disappointed, maybe, but not scared. I, on the other hand, was freaking terrified. I knew from past experience that there's nothing more dangerous or unpredictable than an angry woman, and we were being marched into a whole tribe of them.

We stumbled down the hill, with the women behind us. I looked back over my shoulder a time or two, still amazed at how quickly and efficiently we'd been captured. The sentries both wore moccasins and beaded buckskin shirts over jeans, all designed for furtive movement, and they undoubtedly knew the territory. But I hadn't heard a thing until they were right behind us. I was supposed to be watching Reasons's back, and I hadn't even watched my own.

As we reached the clearing, I thought about running for it. Surely I could outrun these women, though I couldn't remember the last time I'd run anywhere. But I couldn't outrun an arrow or a bullet from my own pistol. Besides, how would I alert Reasons to my plan? Running off and leaving him wouldn't exactly fit the assignment the Ogletroops had given me.

The sentries marched us toward the main house. Women spilled out of the buildings and the tepees to glower at us. Such a gantlet of hate. I figured it had more to do with what hung between our legs than anything we might've actually done.

Some of them wore feathers braided into their hair. Others wore their hair like Judah's, what I've always thought of as the Lesbian Cut, spiky on top and long in the back. Most wore jeans and baggy shirts, but where I could glimpse a bare leg or an armpit, I could see there probably wasn't a razor in the whole compound. That fit with what I guessed were the politics of the place: Shaving is something women do for men, and these women weren't doing anything for men ever again.

Once I started thinking about it like that, I couldn't leave it alone. Two men surrounded by dozens of women, and all I felt was fear. None of the usual lusty looks and puffed-out chests and strutting. Simple, cold fear at being different from everyone around me, and them hating me for it. It reminded me of those few brave blacks who broke down the walls of segregation back home, how scared they must've been, how noble they were in not showing it. Hardly ever in my life had I been part of a minority, and I didn't like it one bit. Nothing noble about the way I sweated and twitched and blinked at the menacing women.

My thoughts must've slowed my feet, because Judah nudged

me in the back with the butt end of the spear to get me moving. Reasons needed no prompting, marching along with his back straight, his eyes directly ahead.

A covered wooden porch was set into the front of the ranch house, and women filled it, drawn outside by the hubbub. Judah ordered us to stop just short of the front steps. The other women massed around us in a rough half circle, blocking all escape, muttering and whispering among themselves.

I was too busy hanging my head to study the women on the porch, but I heard Reasons say, "Hello, Margaret."

I jerked my head up, and there she was, standing with the others on the porch, looking more like her photograph than we'd expected. She still wore her blond hair long, though it hung limp to her shoulders, not sprayed and teased as it had been in her debutante days. She wore a tunic of unbleached cotton, faded jeans, and what looked like enough necklaces and beads to give her a stoop. She didn't seem brainwashed at first glance, her eyes bright and questioning, but she shied at the attention from Reasons, then stepped behind another woman who shielded her protectively.

Her protector, a dark, round gypsy of a woman, stepped forward to the steps and the others edged back from her, giving her room. She clearly was in charge.

"We found these men up the hill, Luna," Judah reported from behind us. "They were spying on the ranch with binoculars, and this one"—she bumped me with her spear—"had a pistol on him."

Judah stepped around me, handed my gun to Luna. She took it as if she'd held one before, no two-fingered squeamishness, and that made me flinch with fear. Of all the ways to die, being shot with my own gun seems the least honorable.

But Luna didn't even point the revolver our way. She let it

dangle by her broad hips while she looked us over. Unlike most of the others, she wore a skirt, a full black number decorated with white stars and half-moons. Her wide-necked purple blouse fell off one bare shoulder, and her dark hair tumbled down her back in a cascade of curls. Her arms were covered with jangling silver bracelets, and she wore a silver stud through one nostril.

Judah yanked our wallets from our hip pockets and handed them over to Luna, who looked inside long enough to check our IDs, then passed them back to Judah, who returned them to us.

"You've been caught trespassing on private land," Luna said brusquely. "State your business."

"We're here to see Margaret Ogletroop," Reasons said before I could open my mouth. "Her family is concerned about her, and they asked us to get a message to her."

Luna turned slightly, looking over her shoulder at a wide-eyed Margaret.

"Margaret? Do you know anything about this?"

"I've never seen these men before in my life."

Luna turned back to us, tried to keep from smiling.

"Seems your story doesn't hold water."

"It's the truth," Reasons said firmly.

"Why would the Ogletroop family hire you two incompetents? Why not just come up here themselves if they want to see Margaret?"

Reasons hesitated, so I jumped in.

"We're both private investigators," I lied. "People hire us to do things they're afraid to do. And Margaret's grandmother is very sick and can't travel up here."

Luna glanced over her shoulder at Margaret, who nodded slightly. She must have known about the Goddess's illness from the family's letters.

"What's the message?" Luna asked.

"We're supposed to tell Margaret her family loves her very much," Reasons said quickly, "and they want her to come home. They're worried about her."

Luna snorted at that. Margaret dropped her eyes.

"Margaret's home is here now," Luna said. "But she's free to come and go as she pleases. If she wants to go to Albuquerque, she should go, and we'll offer a prayer to the goddess that her ailing grandmother will recover."

Margaret's eyes widened at the thought of leaving WOMB.

"Do you want to go with these men, Margaret?"

Margaret shook her head silently, edging farther back into the shadows of the porch.

"There. You see? She doesn't want to go. She's happy here. You've delivered your message, and there's your result."

I cleared my throat.

"Thank you, ma'am. Now, if you'll just call off your people here, we'll be leaving."

Judah poked me with the butt of her spear. Luna smiled.

"Oh, you're not going anywhere," she said. "You were trespassing on our land, and we don't let that go unpunished. If we let you get away with it, every gawker and masher in the state would be up here peeking at us through the trees."

A lump as big as a duck's egg formed in my throat. Reasons apparently had no such problem with fear.

"What do you intend to do with us?"

Luna leaned against a post, crossed her arms over her chest, looked us over, smiling.

"Well, we have lots of options, don't we? I could let Judah and some of her friends strip you naked and chase you through the forest back to wherever you left your car. Let the branches and brambles do our work for us."

A murmur of approval rippled through the women around us.

I glanced around at the thick underbrush. Ouch.

"Or, we could keep you prisoner here, maybe lock you up in the chicken coop. Though I don't think the hens would lay their eggs with two men in their midst."

Reasons didn't flinch. "That would be unlawful imprisonment."

"Oh, it might be considered that way. But you're the intruders, and we have a very healthy relationship with the sheriff's office. I don't think we'd get in much trouble."

Luna stepped away from the post, pointed a stubby finger at us.

"Maybe I'll just put a hex on you. Dry up your testicles. Ruin your eyesight. Make your hair fall out."

Some of the women snickered behind me, and my knees went weak. I don't really believe in magic, but the notion of dried-up testicles was enough to scare me. And I can't afford to lose any more hair.

"You're toying with us," Reasons said. "And I can assure you, we have the inner strength to endure whatever you cook up."

Luna stared hard at him.

"You know, I think you probably do," she said. "Though I don't know about your friend here. He looks worried."

I wanted to respond but couldn't think of anything as stalwart as what Reasons had said. She had me pegged.

"What happened to your eye, anyway?" she asked. "Judah? Did you blacken this man's eye?"

"No," Judah said behind me. "He was that way when we found him."

Luna watched me, waiting for an answer.

"I fell down some stairs."

"Why doesn't that surprise me?"

I shrugged.

"I tell you what we're going to do," she said after a moment's thought. "We're going to call the sheriff and let him arrest you for trespassing."

Several of the women said, "Aawww," disappointed they wouldn't be able to torture us in some way.

"Couldn't you just let us go?" I said quickly. "We won't bother you again."

Luna shook her head.

"Too late. You should've thought about that before you disturbed the serenity of this place."

Over her shoulder, she said, "Selena, get the handcuffs."

One of the amazons disappeared into the house.

"Why would you need handcuffs in a place this serene?" Reasons asked, his mouth curving in a smirk.

"For intruders like you. We can't just stand around here all morning pointing spears at you. We have work to do, blessings to seek from the goddess. Handcuffs will keep you in one place until the sheriff arrives."

She ordered Reasons to sit on the steps at the front of the porch and hug a post, then handcuffed his wrists together. I did the same at another post. It wasn't the most comfortable position, but it beat running naked through the woods.

"Okay, everyone," Luna shouted, "go on about your business. Just ignore these men among us—the way men have enslaved and ignored women throughout history."

The crowd broke up. And, true to Luna's orders, not another woman even looked at us the rest of the morning. We could've been doorstops, for all they noticed. Though doorstops, I imagine, rarely get cramps in their shoulders.

S E V E N

■◆■

Nobody had said Reasons and I couldn't talk while we sat there, but we didn't say much, anyway. We faced opposite directions, making conversation difficult. And we were both too busy stewing in our own juices to chat.

By the time a sheriff's patrol car bounced up the gravel driveway, it was nearly noon, and my stomach was growling. A Hispanic officer, a six-footer about my size, climbed out of the car and sauntered up to where Reasons and I sat silently trussed to the posts. He shifted a toothpick in his mouth as he looked us over.

"This might be the easiest arrest I've ever made."

He wore a tan uniform, a big hogleg in a heavy holster, and a brown baseball cap that had *Sheriff* in yellow letters across the front. The name tag at his breast pocket said, HERNANDEZ.

Luna came out the door in a jangle of bangles, all smiles and confidence. "Good morning, Sheriff."

"Morning, Ms. Luna. Guess you've had a little trouble here."

"These guys? They haven't been much trouble. A couple of

the women spotted them spying on us up there by that dead tree and brought them down to see me. We hated to use the handcuffs, but it was the only way I could think of to keep them still until you got here."

"Excuse me, Sheriff," Reasons spoke up, "but doesn't this qualify as unlawful imprisonment, maybe even kidnapping? You can't just hold people against their will."

Sheriff Hernandez seemed to study that a moment.

"You're not from here, are you, boy?"

Reasons shook his head.

"New Mexico law doesn't think much of trespassers," Hernandez said. "Ms. Luna here would've been within her rights if she'd just shot you once she found you on her property. Compared with that, a little handcuffing doesn't seem so bad to me."

"It's a violation of my constitutional rights!"

I was sending Reasons mental messages that went like this: Shut up! Shut up! Shut up!

Hernandez's eyes narrowed to slits.

"Oh, I see," he said. "We're going strictly by the book here. Making sure everyone's rights stay protected. In that case, I won't even try to work out a compromise between you boys and these women whose privacy you've violated. I'll just run you in."

I twisted my head around to shout over my shoulder, "I'm all for compromise! Let's talk!"

"Too late." Hernandez grinned, enjoying the way Reasons went from all puffed up to deflated at the thought of going to jail. All the air had gone out of my balloon hours ago.

Luna produced keys from the pocket of her skirt, and Hernandez niftily unlocked the handcuffs from one of my wrists, freed me from the pole, then snapped my wrists together again. Once he had Reasons in the same condition, he promised Luna he'd return the cuffs when he was done.

"Oh, no hurry, Sheriff," she said, twinkling at him. "We've got others."

Reasons said acidly, "I'm sure you do. Cults need such tools."

Hernandez gave him a stiff-fingered poke in the chest. "Shut up and get in the car."

After we were in the patrol car, Hernandez talked for a moment with Luna, making arrangements for her to go into Taos and sign a complaint against us. She handed him my gun, which he carried to the car and put in his glove compartment.

If the sheriff was angry, it didn't last long. He hummed to himself as we jounced along down the driveway.

"Pretty spread they've got here, isn't it?" he said to us via the rearview mirror. "Course, you've probably seen more of it than I have, sneaking around in the woods."

He chuckled some more as he steered the car up onto the road.

"We seem to have gotten off on the wrong foot, Sheriff," I said. "We had good reason to be poking around that ranch."

"Is that so? I'd be interested in hearing about that."

Reasons cleared his throat to get my attention, then shook his head when I looked over. I ignored him.

"We were hired by a family to check on one of the women who's living at WOMB. They're worried she's been brainwashed or something. She won't go home. She won't call. We were just trying to get a look at her, make sure she's all right."

Hernandez mulled this over for a moment.

"You see this woman while you were there?"

"Yeah, just for a minute. After they captured us."

"Did she look healthy?"

"Well, yeah."

"Appear to be brainwashed?"

"No, but that's a hard thing to tell at a glance—"

"Doesn't sound like you have much of a case."

"But it's more than simple trespassing. We were on a mission. You can see that."

Hernandez snorted at my choice of words. "On a mission, huh? You two don't look much like missionaries to me."

I thought Reasons looked exactly like a missionary, but I didn't say anything.

"I guess if the girl's family hired you to do this, then maybe they can pay your fines. But if there's jail time to be served, you'll have to do that yourself."

"Jail time? For trespassing?"

"I told you we take it seriously. But you don't have to take my word for it. We'll see what the judge has to say."

My spirits sank. I said nothing more until the sheriff, looking at me in the mirror, asked, "What happened to your eye?"

"Would it help my case if I said those women did this to me?"

"Nope."

"Then I won't lie to you about it. I tipped over in a chair."

"Careless. Would this chair have been at a bar?"

"How did you guess?"

Hernandez grinned. Reasons rolled his eyes at my feeble attempt to ingratiate myself with the sheriff.

"I thought you said you were struck by lightning," he said.

I gave him a shushing look. "White lightning."

That made Hernandez laugh.

As it turned out, cozying up to the sheriff did me no good. As soon as we reached the sheriff's office, which was on the back side of a modern courthouse that looked as if it were made of Legos, he turned us over to a surly booking officer and disappeared into his private office.

Reasons and I kept our mouths shut through the booking process, filling out forms and getting our fingerprints inked. They took all our possessions, Reasons's binoculars, our belts and shoelaces. As if we might hang ourselves for trespassing.

Reasons used his one phone call to ring up Marcus Ogletroop—collect—and tell him our predicament. I couldn't hear Reasons from where I sat, but I could see his face getting redder the longer he talked. Ogletroop clearly wasn't happy with our performance.

The good news was that Reasons and I got a two-bunk cell to ourselves rather than being locked in the drunk tank or some cattle pen with real felons. The bad news was that the clank of the door slamming shut chilled me to my toes.

I'd never been in jail before. In all the times I've played fast and loose with the law, I'd always been able to squirm my way out of trouble before it got this far. Sheriff Hernandez clearly didn't think much of squirming. And I didn't think much of jail.

After the initial shock wore off, I asked Reasons, "So what did Ogletroop say?"

"He said he'd round up his pilot and fly up here right away. He's got a private jet. We should be in here only a couple of hours."

"That's a relief. I take it he wasn't thrilled with us."

"The last thing he wanted was to have the police involved. He doesn't want this in the papers."

That seemed a funny position for someone whose family owned a newspaper, but I didn't say so.

"He cursed at me," Reasons said disgustedly. "Took the Lord's name in vain. I won't stand for blasphemy, I don't care how mad he is."

I still said nothing, but I edged away on my bunk from where Reasons leaned against the concrete wall. Words like *blasphemy* give me the willies. My time in jail might be short, but it would seem a lot longer if Reasons launched into a sermon. I'd just as soon take my chances in the drunk tank.

Fortunately, he let it drop, and we fell into depressed silence. I stretched out on the hard mattress, my hands under my head to protect my hair from whatever critters might live in the linens. Reasons paced up and down a few times, still steamed, then climbed into the top bunk.

We lay like that, bitter sailors in our racks, until a deputy came for us three hours later. He marched us down corridors and into Hernandez's office. Marcus Ogletroop was in a chair near the sheriff's desk, and he rose when we entered.

"Well, you two don't look any worse for wear," he said.

"Oh, they've been very hospitable," Reasons spat. "Can we go now?"

Ogletroop frowned at him.

"As a matter of fact, you can. I've arranged with the sheriff to pay the standard bail without waiting for a hearing before a judge."

"Then let's go."

"Hold on a minute," Hernandez said. "Take a seat."

Reasons and I joined Ogletroop in the hard chairs that formed a half circle around the sheriff's desk.

"Mr. Ogletroop here has explained to me about his sister," Hernandez said. "I understand why he's worried about her. But I want to warn you fellows to stay away from WOMB."

"Don't worry," I said quickly. "We've learned our lesson."

Hernandez grinned.

"Well, I sure hope that's the case. But I find that lessons learned in jail are often forgotten once the perpetrator gets outside. We're too busy around here to keep driving all the way out there when you get caught. So let me put it in concrete terms for you: Don't go bothering those women again. Near as I can tell, they're doing nothing wrong up there at WOMB, and they're not holding anybody against her will.

"We're big on tolerance here in Taos. We don't know a lot about what goes on up at WOMB, to tell you the truth. And we don't care. As long as they don't break any laws, they can pretty much do as they please."

Reasons leaned forward, put his elbows on his knees.

"It's a cult, Sheriff. It has all the classic signs—"

Hernandez silenced him by shaking his head.

"I don't see it that way. Those women are just fed up with men, and they want to be left alone. I can't say I blame them. I get fed up with men sometimes myself, even though I am one."

"That's just the cover they use," Reasons said quickly. "I can guarantee you other things are going on up there. Witchcraft, for instance. Pagan rituals—"

"None of which is illegal," Hernandez said. "Witches have been operating in these mountains since before the white man came. If the women of WOMB think they can tap into those ancient channels, more power to them."

Reasons could see he was getting nowhere. He sat back in his chair with a huff.

"Now, fellas, here's what I really want you to hear," Hernandez said, straightening in his chair. "It might occur to you that you could just waltz into WOMB and snatch Mr. Ogletroop's sister. This would be a very bad idea. First of all, those women up there have plenty of weapons, and they know how to use them, as you two discovered today. Second, I'd come down hard on you. I don't care how worried you might be about her. Taking her out of there against her will would be kidnapping. And a kidnapping charge would keep you inside a cell block for a long, long time. Clear?"

We both nodded silently. Ogletroop seemed impatient, chewing on his lip, looking at his gold wristwatch.

"All right, then." Hernandez sat back, pulled open his middle desk drawer, and produced my revolver. "I'll let Mr. Ogletroop hold on to this while you two check out."

Ogletroop looked uneasy about taking the gun from the sheriff's hand, but Hernandez said, "It's not loaded. I'll be keeping the bullets."

Ogletroop stuffed the gun into the pocket of his sport coat, stood up, and shook the sheriff's hand, thanking him for his cooperation. A deputy arrived to lead Reasons and me off to fetch our shoelaces and wallets.

It was still sunny outside, which disoriented me after my time in the dim jail. Ogletroop waited for us at the curb, next to a shiny rented Range Rover.

"Get in."

We obeyed. Reasons took the front seat, and I spread out in the back. It was a luxurious vehicle, with wood paneling on the dash and leather upholstery on the seats. Ogletroop slammed it into gear and we lurched off down the street.

"I can't believe you guys," he sputtered. "Less than one day on the job, and already I'm bailing you out of jail. I thought you understood we wanted to keep this quiet."

I knew to remain silent, but Reasons apparently had less experience with being browbeaten.

"We tried to—"

"Shut up. I don't want to hear your excuses. If it were up to me, I'd leave you in that jail to rot. Unfortunately, my grandmother still thinks you two geniuses will come up with something."

I said a silent prayer of thanks to the Goddess. I'd finally found a case that could make me some money. I needed the solid backing of somebody until I could get it sorted out. Marcus Ogletroop clearly wasn't that somebody, but I could count on the Goddess.

After Ogletroop stewed awhile, he spoke up again.

"So, did you even get a look at Margaret?"

The question hung there a second, neither of us wanting to be the first to answer. Finally, I gave it a try.

"Yes, we did. She looked healthy and happy, though she seemed sort of cowed by the woman who runs the place."

"Do you think there's any chance of getting her out of there?"

"Sure, but the sheriff said—"

"I don't care what he said. I want Margaret away from that place, the sooner the better."

"I understand that, but maybe we ought to let things cool down for a day or two. The sheriff—"

Reasons cut me off. He seemed to have a knack for saying the wrong thing at the right time.

"We can get her," he said. "It's just a matter of watching the place, and waiting for the right opportunity. I think you're correct. The sooner we get her away from WOMB, the sooner we can get her thinking straight again."

We pulled into the parking lot of the Holiday Inn and Ogletroop stopped the car.

"That's what I want," he said grimly. "Get the job done."

What could I say other than "Yes, sir"?

"And don't get caught again. I can't be dropping everything and flying up to Taos just because you two can't outrun a bunch of skirts in the woods."

He handed me my gun, looked at his watch again, and muttered something about being late for a board meeting. Reasons and I jumped out of the car and managed to get the doors closed before he roared away.

We stood there in the parking lot, watching him go.

"You sure sounded confident, telling him we could snatch Margaret out of WOMB," I said.

Reasons smiled primly.

"I am confident. We have God on our side."

E I G H T
■ ◆ ■

Legislators love to declare items the "official" symbols of their states. All states have official flowers (New Mexico's is the towering yucca) and birds (the roadrunner). But it seems that lately some places have taken it to extremes, declaring official state trees and official state fish and official state mammals and official state campaign contributors. In New Mexico, we have an official state cookie (the *bizcochito*) and an official state fossil (some junior dinosaur).

What they should declare is an official state vehicle—the pickup truck. New Mexico must have more pickups per capita than anywhere in the world: little Japanese trucks, low-rider trucks, battered old swaybacked trucks, shiny monster trucks with giant tires and more lights than a prison tower. Part of it stems from the state's heritage of ranching, where pickups have replaced cowboys' horses. Rural lifestyles require trucks for hauling and towing and slogging through muddy pastures. But city folk drive them, too. In a boomtown like Albuquerque, every third vehicle seems to be a pickup full of construction equipment.

And the rest are owned by attorneys and accountants and actuaries, who feel very macho behind the wheel of an overpowered truck, sitting up higher than the rest of us on the freeway.

I wouldn't have one myself. Tailing people requires a low-profile vehicle like my old Chevy, a car you can hide behind a hedge, one that doesn't get a second glance from passersby.

With pickups being everywhere, it's a tall order to find one that tried to kill you.

But I'm getting ahead of myself here. After Ogletroop roared away, Reasons and I decided to get some food. We hadn't eaten all day. We'd arrived at the jail too late for whatever culinary delight they'd served at noontime, which probably was just as well.

Reasons's rental car was still up the valley where we'd left it, so we took my Chevy into the center of town and found a café that was serving in late afternoon. Since I was starving, I let it all hang out, ordering a steak and fries, a beer, coffee, a slice of apple pie. Reasons requested a bowl of vegetable soup.

"You a vegetarian?" I asked him after the waitress took our orders.

"Let's just say I try not to devour any more of God's creatures than necessary," he said smugly.

"Aren't vegetables God's creations, too?"

"Yes, but I don't think they have souls."

"Neither does beef."

"How do you know?"

"You ever spent any time around cows? Look in one's eyes sometime. They barely have brains, much less souls."

"I'm not sure brains and souls have that much to do with each other."

"You can say that again."

"The least educated sometimes are the most spiritual. I've seen retarded people who are blissfully close to God."

"Too dumb to doubt."

Reasons frowned at me. "You've really closed yourself off to God, haven't you, Bubba?"

"Not entirely. I still catch myself saying little mental prayers from time to time. Usually when I'm in trouble."

"No atheists in foxholes, eh?"

"Ever notice how few foxholes you encounter in day-to-day life?"

"I don't know. I felt like we were in one this morning, up at WOMB. God saw us through that."

"If He'd been paying better attention, maybe we wouldn't have been caught at all."

Reasons was nervous in the face of so much bitter disbelief. His hands picked at each other on the tabletop.

"Whatever the reason," he said slowly, "we certainly haven't made much progress. And we've lost the element of surprise. Those women know we'll be back."

"You think so? I thought I put on a pretty convincing show of being scared of them."

"It was convincing all right. Are you a Method actor? You really seemed to be getting into that role."

"Ooh, what's that I smell? Is there sarcasm in the air?"

The waitress arrived with our food. I sawed off a big bite of steak and shoved it into my mouth, feeling reckless and guilt-free. Reasons ignored me, closing his eyes and moving his lips in a silent blessing over the food. Maybe he was commending the cow's soul to heaven. I didn't care. I'd been around the sanctimonious little shit for less than twenty-four hours, and already I'd had my fill. It was becoming increasingly difficult to imagine us working together.

Keep thinking about the money, I told myself. You can put up with a lot for a thousand bucks. And setbacks like the one we'd had at WOMB meant it all could take longer and cost the

Ogletroops more. They were my gravy train, and I couldn't get derailed by Reasons's piety.

After we'd eaten in silence awhile, Reasons said, "So, Bubba, what do you think we should do next?"

"Well, I was just thinking our first order of business should be retrieving your rental car. Then we need to scout the area around WOMB some more. There's got to be a better way to get onto that property than the route we took today. That ranch is shaped like a bowl, and it's easy for them to watch the sides from down where they're sitting."

"Maybe we should make our move at night."

The thought of prowling snake-infested forests after dark made me instantly anxious.

"No good," I said quickly. "We don't even know where Margaret sleeps. We can't just go peeking in windows until we find her. What we need to do is stake the place out and watch for a while. Like anybody else, they have routines, some of which may isolate Margaret from the rest of them."

"They're probably watching her closely now," he said. "In case we come back. And they're weighing whether our appearance has caused her to doubt her choices."

"Maybe it will. Maybe all that talk about her grandmother being sick will get her to go see her family."

Reasons shook his head. "She's in too deep. I could see it in her eyes."

I shrugged. "You never can tell."

"I can tell."

I fought off the urge to roll my eyes.

"Maybe we ought to talk to that rancher up there, Valdez," I said. "He might know of some way to approach their property without getting caught."

I told Reasons about the clipping Felicia had supplied, about how Valdez had blamed the WOMBsters for his cattle mutilations. Reasons looked a little too fascinated for my liking.

"It's possible he's right," he said. "Pagans often use animals or animal parts in their sacrifices."

"Seems to me plenty of animals up in those woods would be easier to bring down than a cow. A nice squirrel or something would probably mean just as much to their goddess."

Now it was Reasons's turn to shrug. "Who can say what they're thinking? Once you get caught up in an aberrant belief system, rational decision making is no longer a priority. Look at Jonestown or Waco. You think if Jim Jones or David Koresh had said, 'Go and bring me a cow's udder,' their people would've questioned it for a second?"

I shook my head.

"This seems like a very different sort of group to me."

"Only in degree, Bubba. If that."

After we finished eating, we returned to the Chevy. It flooded out when I tried to start it, and I spent five minutes cranking at it before the engine finally caught. Reasons sat silently in the passenger seat, looking smug, as if he thought God were having His vengeance on me through my carburetor.

Daylight was waning by the time we reached the rental car, but it was still easy to see that all four tires were flat. Reasons went stiff beside me, but he said nothing. He climbed out of my car and walked around the rental, squatting to examine the deflated tires.

"They're not slashed," he said when he returned to the Chevy. "Someone just let all the air out at the valves."

"Someone? I think we can make a pretty good guess who it might've been. The WOMBsters are probably watching us right now, getting a big old belly laugh at our expense."

Reasons glanced around at the darkening woods as if he expected to spot skulking women, then hunched his shoulders.

"Doesn't seem like much of a joke to me," he said. "But I guess they felt the need for revenge since Luna wouldn't let them torture us. God will forgive them. It's a pretty small sin."

I practically had to chew off my own tongue, but I didn't say anything.

I'd kept the Chevy's engine running, and I turned it around and headed back into Taos. The rental-car office was closing, but Reasons talked his way inside so they could fill out whatever forms were needed and send a repair truck to fetch the crippled car.

While he was inside, I spotted an army-navy store down the block. I locked up the Chevy, then angled across the street to the store. The door jingled as I went inside. The place was the typical jumble of camping gear and boots and ropes and Swiss army knives.

A bearded, sunburned young man with enough dark hair to share some with me stood behind the counter, listlessly leafing through a skiing magazine. He would have a long wait until the ski slopes opened up again, and he looked like everything else in life bored him.

The glass case he leaned his elbows on was filled with various sizes and types of binoculars, and I squatted to peer in at them, bracing myself for a sales pitch that never came. Each set was labeled with its magnification strength and price, so I didn't really need any help, anyway. I settled on an olive drab pair set in a thick rubber case. Compact and cheap, but powerful enough for me to see everything I'd need to up at WOMB. I stood up, cleared my throat to show I was ready, and told the clerk which pair I wanted. He wordlessly retrieved it from the case, rang up the sale, took my money, and put the binoculars in a sack for me.

The whole transaction had taken maybe two minutes. When I stepped out on the sidewalk, there was still no sign of Reasons by the Chevy. I waited at the curb until a Volvo passed, then glanced both ways and stepped down onto the street. A deep-throated engine roared to life down the block.

A big old pickup truck with rattling ladder racks roared out of its parking space and drove straight at me. I froze like a possum, the glare of the headlights blinding me. The truck bore down on me, straddling the yellow stripe in the middle of the street. I didn't know which way to jump, but I quickly settled on backward.

I wheeled, took two steps, then launched myself toward the sidewalk, cradling my new binoculars in my arms like a football. My knee hit the asphalt first, then my shoulder as I rolled up against the curb. The truck's tires passed inches from my nose. I could smell the rubber as the pickup screeched away.

The truck careened down the street, then disappeared around a corner.

I pulled myself up onto the curb, just in case the driver decided to make the block, and felt my knees, shoulders, and elbows, looking for telltale lumps that might signal a broken bone. Everything seemed to be where it belonged. I shimmied the leg of my jeans up over my knee to see whether it had been scraped clean of hide, but the old denim had done its job, and my skin was red but unbroken.

"Bubba! What are you doing?"

It was Reasons, calling from across the street. I must've looked curious, sitting on the curb like a wino, one pants leg hitched up, my pale leg sticking out.

"Didn't you see it?" I shouted back. "Someone tried to run me down!"

"What?"

I shook my head to signal, Never mind. Creaking to my feet, I picked up my package from the curb. I made sure no cars were coming for as far as I could see, then hobbled across the street to where he waited by the Chevy.

"Someone tried to run me down. A pickup truck, gray or light blue—hard to tell in this light—with ladder racks on the back."

"Are you hurt?"

"Naw, just shook up. My heart's beating faster than an oversexed rabbit's."

Reasons frowned. "Think we should report it to the police?"

"And say what? That I was jaywalking, and nearly got run over? I don't even know what make of truck it was. I was too busy getting out of the way. It was all headlights and deadly tires, as near as I could tell."

"Maybe it was an accident. You *were* crossing in the middle of the block—"

"It was no accident. The truck was parked down the way there. When I went to step into the street, the engine fired up and it headed straight for me. Whoever was in that truck must've been following us."

"You think so?" Reasons almost grinned. "Think we've attracted that much attention already?"

"Maybe so. I haven't been watching the mirrors. It hadn't occurred to me that we might've picked up a tail."

"What were you doing over there anyway?"

"Buying these." I opened the sack and removed the binoculars from their case. They were still intact. "You won't be the only one getting a good view when we go back up to WOMB. And I'll be looking for a pickup with ladder racks."

N I N E

■◆■

Jeronimo Valdez was a squat man with a face as brown and burnished as an old saddle. He sat in a rocking chair on the deep, shadowy front porch of his adobe home, but he rocked to his feet when we pulled up out front in the Chevy. He stepped to the front of the porch, into the sunlight, and pushed a battered straw cowboy hat back on his head. He looked us over as we got out of the car and then, as if in appraisal, spat a stream of tobacco juice into the dirt.

"You boys lost?"

"No, sir," I said, "we've come to see Mr. Valdez."

"You're looking at him. What can I do for you?"

Reasons hung back, sensing, for once, that his Yankee accent and manner were out of place here and that he should let me do the talking.

"Well, sir, we're looking into your neighbors, those women down in the valley, and we thought you could answer some questions for us."

Valdez chewed on that for a second, then spat again.

"You the police?"

"No, sir. Private detectives."

"I was hoping you were the police. I've reported those women time and again, but I can't get anybody to take it serious."

"We're serious as a heart attack. Tell us about it."

Valdez jerked his head toward the house, an unspoken invitation up onto the porch. I followed him into the shade and sat on an old ladder-back chair. He took the rocker, leaving Reasons to plunk himself down on the steps. An ancient hound waggled up to him, sniffing and drooling. Reasons looked alarmed.

"Does he bite?"

Valdez cackled.

"He ain't got enough teeth left in his old head to bite anybody. About like me."

He opened his mouth in a wide grin, showing a mouth like a jack-o'-lantern, every other tooth long gone, the remaining ones yellowed by tobacco.

"You boys want some coffee?"

"That'd be nice."

The old man shouted a stream of Spanish through the open door.

In truth, I'd had plenty of coffee already, enough that I'd be stopping behind every tree between here and WOMB. Reasons had awakened me early, eager to get going, but I was stiff and creaky from dodging the pickup truck the night before, and I had insisted on breakfast and several cups of coffee to lubricate me before I would head toward WOMB. But a private eye knows never to turn down the offer of a beverage during an interview. If a person suddenly decides he doesn't want to talk to you, a cup of coffee or a glass of whiskey gives you reason to linger. It's worked for me before.

While we waited for the coffee, Valdez stared off into the distance. The land rolled away in all directions, partially cleared of

71

trees and brush, grass lush from spring rains. The road dead-ended in front of his house, but a rutted dirt track jutted off to the west, slithering under a gate and climbing the ridge.

"See that track? That runs up along that ridge to my west pastures. Right above the old Bankhead ranch. It was up there that I found a couple of my heifers butchered."

"Butchered?"

"Mutilated. Eyes, udders, and assholes cut away clean as a whistle. They left the rest, perfectly good beef ruined from being out in the sun all day before I found them."

Valdez picked up a can from beside his rocking chair and spewed a stream of tobacco juice into it. All his busy chewing made me want a cigarette, an urge that still hits me occasionally, though I quit smoking years ago.

A beautiful dark girl of maybe twenty appeared in the doorway with three cups of steaming coffee on a tray. Valdez's eyes lit up at the sight of her.

"Ah! This is my daughter, Juanita."

The girl kept her eyes averted, shy. We each took a cup from the tray and she disappeared back into the house.

"The last of my children to live here," Valdez said. "All the others have moved away, gone to the big city to make their fortunes. I work the ranch by myself, and Juanita looks after the house."

I nodded but said nothing, waiting for him to get back to the cattle-mutilation story.

"Not many ranches left up here," he said. "Everything's been turned over to the *turistas*, and people like those women down the road."

"How long they been living over there?"

Valdez squinted, thinking.

"Guess it's been three years now. My papa used to own that parcel. Wasn't worth much as grazing land because it's too steep, but it does have that creek running through it. Anyway, he sold

72

it to old man Bankhead better'n fifty years ago. Needed the money, and he figured letting a painter live down there was better than turning it over to the bank."

Valdez paused to finger the tobacco out of his cheek into the can. Then we all drank coffee in unison. It was hot and strong and sugarless.

"Bankhead never caused us any trouble, was a good neighbor. But he died years ago, and the family kind of let the place go to seed. Then, a few years ago, his daughter showed up on the place. What's her name?"

He seemed to have gotten stuck on this point, so I helped him out, remembering the name in the clippings. "Vivian?"

"Yeah, that's right, Vivian. She's a strange one. Never married, though she's got to be in her forties. She was old man Bankhead's youngest. Anyway, she moved back onto the ranch, and pretty soon all sorts of women started showing up over there."

"You get to know any of them?"

"Nah, I keep to myself up here, and I want my neighbors to do the same. But I did notice all the coming and going, heard them hammering together those new buildings over there."

"When did the cattle turn up dead?"

"Oh, that was much later, about six months ago now. Two heifers, within a week of each other. The cops tried to tell me buzzards got to them, but I've seen the work of buzzards before, and this was something else.

"I couldn't prove those women were responsible for it, or else I would've gone down to visit them with my shotgun. So I did the only other thing I could think of. I made a lot of noise about it—to the cops, to the newspapers. None of my heifers has gone missing since."

He nodded, still congratulating himself on his strategy.

"What makes you so sure your neighbors did it?"

"It's the only thing that makes any sense. Only one road into those pastures, and you have to drive right by here to get there. We didn't see anybody going in or out. But that pasture is just up the hill from them, a short hike. Besides, they do strange things over there. This seemed to fit."

Reasons finally spoke up from the steps, where he sat with his coffee cup in one hand and the hound's ear in the other. "What kinds of strange things have you witnessed?"

"Witnessed? I haven't witnessed anything. Like I said, I keep to myself. But I hear things, drumming, chanting. And, once, when I was over in those woods looking for a heifer I thought had jumped the fence, I saw some kind of altar. Big thing made outta flat rocks, with feathers and buffalo skulls and other shit hanging all over it."

"Was anybody worshiping at this altar?"

"Not when I was there. I took one look at that thing and high-tailed it out of there, saying Hail Marys all the way back to the house."

Reasons and I nodded, sipped our coffee. The time had come for asking favors, but I wasn't sure where to begin with Valdez. The West is known for its hospitality, just like the South, and there's plenty of truth to that. But I was about to propose crossing fences and driving in pastures, and that, according to many westerners, would be going too far. The land is inviolate. When an entire economy had been based for generations on the land and what it could offer, people guard it jealously. Take my money, elope with my daughter, but leave my land alone.

I told Valdez about the day before, how we'd slithered down the hillside right into the clutches of WOMB. I made it sound more comic and less terrifying than it had really been, and he had a good laugh at our expense. Then he set his coffee cup on a nearby windowsill and carved another chaw off a plug of Day's Work with a sharp little penknife. Once he was settled in with his tobacco, he spoke up.

"I get the feeling you boys want some help."

"Yes, sir, we do," I said before Reasons could shake off the offer. "We were hoping you'd allow us to use that track there."

I gestured toward the dirt ruts with my chin in my best faux-rancher method.

"We'd like to drive up on that ridge and find another way down into the valley, one where we wouldn't be so obvious. And then we want to watch those women some more to see if we can figure out a way of cutting one out of the herd."

I felt like patting myself on the back for that bit of down-home imagery, but Valdez didn't even smile, too busy nodding and thinking it over.

"How long would this take?"

"Couple of days, maybe. We'd let ourselves in, if that's all right with you, and we'll be sure to close the gate."

"You won't spook my cattle?"

"No, sir."

"All right, then, I'll tell you what you do. Follow that track up onto the ridge. When it starts to dip back down toward the valley, stop right there. If you look close, you'll see an old trail that runs down the hillside by a big rock outcrop. Follow that on down into the valley. You'll be screened off from their houses by those rocks. The trail will take you down to where they've dammed up the creek, on the far side of the ranch. They won't be expecting anybody to come down that way 'cause it's so far from the road."

Reasons and I got to our feet, me thanking Valdez for his time and the coffee.

"I've got one question," Reasons said over my shushing looks. "If you don't ever go over there, how do you know about this trail?"

Valdez's face creased into a gap-toothed smile.

"That trail's been there since I was a boy. I used to sneak down that hill to go skinny-dipping while my papa thought I was minding the herd. A small sin, no?"

We all had a laugh over that, and I hustled Reasons off to the Chevy before he could make any more conversation. We bumped along the track to the gate, and Reasons jumped out of the car and fumbled the gate open and latched it behind us.

It was all as Valdez had said. Just before the dirt track began to dip back down toward the valley in a washed-out tangle, we parked and located the old trail. Limbs and brush reached across it, but the footpath was packed bare earth and the going was easy. The trail followed the edge of the granite outcrop, which was easily two stories high and encrusted with lichens. Here and there, we had to step over boulders that had given way and plopped onto the trail.

We were better prepared this time around. I wore a dark denim shirt instead of one that was so obvious, and I had the binoculars and my pistol on my belt. Reasons carried his binoculars and a canteen of water. It was just a matter of padding along down the hillside, finding a vantage point, and setting up for the day. Still, we moved slowly and paused occasionally to listen for any sign that spear-chucking power lifters might be nearby.

We heard the women before we saw them. High-pitched squeals and laughter and splashing. Reasons and I edged along, crouched and ready to run, until we reached the bottom of the outcrop, where it petered away into a tumble of boulders and pines.

After a whispered conference, I crawled on ahead, stealthy as a hunter, while Reasons scanned the area, watching for guards. I slipped behind a tree when I got my first glimpse of water, then squirmed around in the brush until I could see to the east, where the water pooled behind a dam made of old railroad timbers.

Oh, my, what a sight. Through the binoculars, I found a dozen women going for a swim in the waist-deep pool, giggling and splashing one another, feeling free to frolic without the eyes of men on them or the chafing of swimsuits. It was every voyeur's dream, nude women lounging on big flat rocks, jumping into the pool, diving underwater, their white behinds flashing for an instant like the backs of dolphins.

I remembered what I was supposed to be there for, and I signaled Reasons to come on over. He came toward me on his hands and knees, and I stopped watching his slow progress in favor of the view through the glasses. I spotted Margaret Ogletroop as she climbed, glistening, out of the pool, her blond hair a wet rope down her back, her arms crossed shyly over her breasts as she jounced to where she'd left her towel. Luna was close behind her, all dripping ringlets and pendulous breasts, her lascivious laughter ringing through the trees.

Reasons appeared at my elbow, and I silently pointed to where Margaret and Luna had gone. He lay on the opposite side of the big pine I was hiding behind, and trained his binoculars on them.

I watched, too, as Luna toweled off Margaret's back and wrung out her hair. Margaret smiled at these ministrations, then turned to return the favor. I felt a knot in my throat, and a harder one in my jeans, as I watched the two women touching each other. When they were dry, Luna took Margaret's hand and led her through the trees. We lost them from view for a few minutes, but they reappeared on the other side of a grove of trees, farther from us but still visible in a little tree-ringed meadow dotted with white flowers. They spread their towels on the grass and sat down close to each other, smiling and whispering.

Reasons shifted on the other side of the pine, getting a better view.

Luna started braiding Margaret's long hair, with Margaret's back nuzzled up close to her. But Luna soon lost interest in her braiding project, more intent on kissing Margaret's bare shoulders and cupping her breasts in her hands. Margaret turned her head so their mouths could meet, and they kissed long and deeply. Luna squeezed Margaret's breasts, then let her hands slowly trail down her stomach toward the dark triangle between her legs.

My heart hammered in my chest, and my mouth was dry. So were my eyes, since I hadn't blinked in minutes. Reasons suddenly stirred beside me.

"I can't watch this," he whispered. Then he was on his feet and moving away, tripping over rocks, not even trying to be quiet.

I could watch all day, I thought, but I had no choice but to follow him. I took one more glance through the glasses, saw Luna pulling Margaret down on the towels to lie beside her, and then I got to my feet and scrambled off to catch up to Reasons.

T E N

■ ◆ ■

Reasons was halfway up the steep trail before I caught up with him. I called to him several times in a stage whisper, but he ignored me, his shoulders hunched, his feet moving determinedly. I trotted a few steps and grabbed his shoulder, spun him around.

"Get your hands off me!" he hissed. His face was dark with rage or shame and his eyes looked as if they could brim over with tears. I was so taken aback that I snatched my hand back and sidled away from him. He turned on his heel and marched on up the hillside.

I hung back, torn between following him and returning to our surveillance spot. He couldn't leave without me; I had the car keys in my pocket. And how often does a man stumble upon a peep show like the one we'd left? Plus, we were definitely learning more about Margaret Ogletroop and her attachment to WOMB. Finally, though, I allowed Reasons to prevail and followed him up the hill, sighing and muttering to myself about missed opportunities.

Reasons was sitting in the Chevy's passenger seat when I arrived, his eyes straight ahead, his mouth clamped shut. I cranked up the engine without a word, turned the car around, and bumped back toward the Valdez place.

Valdez's porch was empty as we passed the house, though I thought I glimpsed his daughter's dark silhouette move away from a window. The asphalt road in Arroyo Seco was a relief after the rutted gravel road, and I sped along, wondering what was eating Reasons. We were halfway back to town before I finally spoke up.

"You want to tell me what that was all about? We went to a lot of trouble to get to the perfect surveillance spot, we're there fifteen minutes, and then you've got to leave."

Reasons shook his head slightly, as if my question were a fly buzzing in his ear.

"Well?"

"We have to be very careful," he said quietly. "We can't allow ourselves to be dragged into sin."

"What sin?"

"Lust. Envy."

"Look, pal, lust is my middle name. I spend half my life peeking in windows at people who are madly humping away. I take their pictures. I show the pictures to their spouses. It all gets ugly, and I get paid. If you don't have the stomach for it, why don't you bail out and let me handle this myself?"

Reasons pondered that.

"Maybe we both should pull out," he said. "What we saw changes everything. If Margaret Ogletroop is in love with that woman, then it'll be nearly impossible to win her over."

"I don't care about winning her over to anything. I only care about getting her out of there and collecting my money."

"That's all this is about for you? Money?"

"That's right." I wasn't sure that was exactly true anymore. I was getting caught up in the Ogletroop family woes. And I was trying to impress Felicia with my detective skills. But the money was the main thing.

Reasons's blank face twisted into a scowl.

"Then I'll have to stick with it," he said. "God needs a representative here."

"Well, I wish He'd sent one who wouldn't turn tail and run at the first sign of a little lesbo kissy-face."

Reasons's head jerked away like I'd slapped him. He stared out the window at the passing houses and said no more.

Perhaps I was too hard on the guy. We shared a planet, but we inhabited different worlds. In his, sin and faith were palpable conditions, all overseen by an active, involved God. In my world, centered along Central Avenue, sin was an opinion, a matter of degree. One man's sin was another man's bread and butter. And faith? Well, let's just say exposure to enough crime and death and deprivation gives you the feeling that nobody's watching. And, if nobody's looking, then why not do what feels good at the moment?

"Look, Reasons," I said finally, "I don't mean to be so hard on you. But you knew this was going to be weird going in, and that's the way it's turning out. Way weird. If we're going to get Margaret out of there, we may have to do things we normally wouldn't do."

He said nothing, wouldn't look at me.

"I tell you what," I said. "Let me buy you some lunch. We can talk it over some more, figure out some strategy. Okay?"

He took a long time to come around, but finally he nodded, and muttered, "I have to stop by my room first. There's something I must do."

I agreed, tried to joke around with him a little, but he was like stone. We arrived at the Holiday Inn, and I parked in front of his room, which was just a few doors down from mine.

"You want me to wait in the car?"

"I don't care."

I shrugged, popped open the door, and followed him inside. His room was quite a contrast to mine, everything in Spartan order, nothing lying out for the maids to pilfer. My room, like my room in Albuquerque, was a jumble of dirty clothes and loose change and half-empty Coke cans.

Reasons headed straight into the bathroom and closed the door. I flopped into a chair, switched on the TV, and flipped through channels without finding anything to catch my attention. Minutes crawled past, and Reasons still didn't come out. My stomach growled, and my impatience grew. Finally, I went over to the bathroom door and listened. From inside, I heard what I took to be a familiar sound, a rapid *slap-slap-slapping*. The guy was jerking off! All that talk about lust and sin, and he was in there whipping his wombat!

I pressed my ear tighter against the door. My weight against it caused the door to swing open. I almost fell inside, but I caught myself, rocked back on my heels by what I saw.

"What the hell—"

Reasons squatted sweatily on the closed lid of the toilet, shirtless, a lash made from a thin, knotted rope in his hand. His bare back was covered with tiny bloody welts. His eyes were filled with tears.

"Get out!"

"What are you doing?"

"Purging evil thoughts. You wouldn't understand. Now get out of here."

I stumbled backward, my head reeling. I closed the door with a bang, then wandered around the motel room for a minute, trying to collect myself. Purvis Reasons was even stranger than I'd thought. What kind of fanatic would believe God wants him to whale the tar out of himself just because he glimpsed a little bare flesh?

One thing I knew for certain. I didn't want to be hanging around when Reasons came out of that bathroom. I let myself out the door, closed it behind me, and beat it the hell out of there.

E L E V E N
■ ◆ ■

I didn't see Reasons again that day. In fact, I didn't do much of anything. I thought about going back out to WOMB alone, but inertia took hold and I ended up whiling away the afternoon in front of a televised baseball game. I don't even like baseball.

The sun was going down by the time I broke out of my stupor. I might've sat there in front of the TV all evening, lost in my thoughts about God and women and Reasons and money, had it not been for the hunger pangs. I had to eat. I needed to get up and move around. It was Saturday night, I was in a strange town, and there was no reason to mope my way into bed.

I put on a fresh shirt and went out to the Chevy. Down the way, the windows of Reasons's room were dark. I was tempted to knock, to try to drag him out of his guilty funk and into some nightlife. But I recognized my motivation as selfishness, not charity. He was the only person I knew in Taos, and even an uneasy evening of churchy chatter would beat dining alone. But I cranked up the Chevy and drove away, leaving Reasons to his penance.

I turned south onto the highway, away from the center of town, and drove a mile or so to where the Sagebrush Inn stood like the old adobe stagecoach stop it once had been. The dusty parking lot was packed, but I found a place to leave the Nova, and scuffed to the front door of the rambling building.

Inside, the place was a noisy bustle. Giant oil paintings of Indians hung on the plaster walls, looking down on locals in their best western wear, families with squirming children and tourists who looked dressed for golf in their Ban-Lons and Sansabelts. The dining room was huge, filled with heavy tables and decorated with Navajo rugs and pottery and cacti.

I asked a pretty dark-eyed hostess for a table for one, and she seated me by a window, where I could look out at sunset shadows creeping down the mountains surrounding town.

The steak and potatoes were perfect, but I didn't pay much attention to the food, too busy sneaking looks at the smiling couples seated nearby. The Sagebrush apparently was the hot spot for big dinner dates, and it felt awkward and lonely to be sitting by myself. I thought about Felicia, about how I hadn't even called her since I'd arrived in Taos, about how much fun we'd have if she was here with me. That only made me feel worse.

By the time I'd wolfed down my food, I was in a black humor, one that could only be cured by a healthy slug of bourbon. I paid my tab and asked the waitress about a bar. She looked at me quizzically, then told me there was one right there in the building. It was the most popular spot in town, she said, and the country-western band would be tuning up about now.

Normally, I'd just as soon listen to a dentist's drill as country music. But here in the surroundings of the Sagebrush, with the Old West all around me, it seemed like the perfect antidote for the blues.

The bar and dining room were connected by a narrow L-shaped corridor—no wonder I hadn't noticed it when I arrived—

and other people were drifting that way, too, burping and picking their teeth after consuming their portions of beef. Reasons would hate this place, I mused, with all its animal souls flying to heaven on the smoke from the grill.

The corridor emptied into the saloon between the bar and a small stage that rose in a corner. A trio of cowboy types was tuning up, and the small dance floor was crowded with couples standing around talking, ready to two-step the night away. I bought a double bourbon at the bar, then threaded my way between tables to the back of the room, putting as much space between me and the band as possible.

Once I was seated at a tiny round table, I scoped out the room, which was long and narrow and decorated to its high rafters in southwestern kitsch—cow skulls and Indian rugs and pottery and carved saints. Near my table, an ancient saddle straddled a sawhorse. I wondered how many drunken cowboys had tried to ride the thing home over the years.

The band struck up its first song, and the dance floor became a swirl of color, all swinging skirts and bobbing cowboy hats and dangerous elbows. The dancers were packed tightly together, but all seemed to be moving more or less in the same direction, counterclockwise, so the chance of collision was slim.

Country-western dancing remains all the rage in these parts. Women love all that touching and twirling, and even the ugliest cowpoke can get a date if he can do the two-step, a schottische, and the Cotton-Eyed Joe. It's such a big part of Albuquerque's social life that even Felicia has wanted to try it. I refuse to play along. All those steps and hitches and twists would have me stumbling over my big feet in no time. She swears it's not that complicated, but to me it's as foreign and elaborate as fencing, and probably more hazardous.

About the only way for a nondancer to stay amused in a dance bar is to watch the efforts of the bad dancers doing their best to pick up women. As I sipped my second bourbon, I settled on one old boy who was having a rough time of it. He was nothing special, average size, bit of a beer gut, with a nose that looked like it had been broken at least twice. He wore a tall white Resistol hat and a western shirt decorated with cowboys and horses, like something a kid would wear to bed. The most noticeable thing about him was his boots, round-toed ropers the color of turquoise. Something about the man—probably those boots— turned off the women. He'd go up to a table full of them, select the one he wanted to dance with, turn on the charm, and then look crestfallen when he got rejected. But after a minute or two, he'd prop that smile up, move along to another table, and try it all over again.

When some woman agreed, he turned out to be not much of a dancer, clumsy and dogged, sweating through his shirt with the effort. Exactly like I'd be, I decided. The difference was that he was ever optimistic, as if his abilities would magically improve and a woman would agree to a second dance. As long as I was watching, neither happened. He was well on his way to having danced with, or been rejected by, every woman in the crowded saloon by the time I called it a night and departed for the Holiday Inn.

Something about old Blue Boots made me feel better about myself. I might be stuck on a case, with a religious nut for a partner, but at least I wasn't making a jackass out of myself for all the world to see. I sucked in lungfuls of the cool night air as I walked out to the Chevy, paused to stare up into a star-littered sky, and found myself actually humming. Could this be a good mood settling over me for a change? Or was it just the bourbon?

The windows of Reasons's room were still dark when I pulled into the parking lot. I couldn't tell whether he was in there, and I wasn't about to knock. Let him work out his demons in private. I parked squarely in front of my room, with the headlights shining on my door, and saw, before I even got out of the car, that the door was ajar, pulled shut but not latched. Hair tingled on the back of my neck. I'd locked that door. I was sure of it.

I got my revolver out of the glove compartment, checked the cylinder even though I knew I'd loaded it that morning. Then I stepped out of the Chevy and tiptoed up to the door of my room, keeping to one side in case gunshots suddenly burst from it. Nothing happened.

I reached my free hand out to push open the door, my gun cocked and ready in the other. No sound came from the darkened room. Something occurred to me, and I called out, "Reasons?" Nothing.

I jumped across the doorway, exposing myself for a second, pressed my back against the wall between the door and window. Nothing. I reached inside, found the light switch, flipped it on.

Somebody had been in my room, but they weren't there now. A dresser drawer hung open. The top of the dresser, which had been covered with dirty underwear and coins, was raked clean. The bed, freshly made that morning by the maid, was rumpled, as if someone had turned down the covers and put them back roughly.

I edged into the room, checked the closet and the bathroom, my breath coming hard. Nobody.

I carried my puzzlement back into the bedroom, started to sit on the edge of the bed and sort it out. But I noticed a lump under the bedspread. The pillows were present and accounted for up by the headboard. Whoever had broken into my room had left me a present in the middle of the bed.

My heart pounding, I stepped to the side of the bed and gently grasped the top of the bedspread. Bracing for anything, my gun at the ready, I threw back the covers to find a huge goddamn rattlesnake in the bed, coiled, ready to strike.

"Aaaaaaiiieee!" *Bam! Bam! Bam! Bam!*

My gun jumped in my hand without any signal from my brain. At least one of the bullets hit the snake, but the others tore into the mattress, throwing clumps of foam into the air, burning black holes in the sheet. But there was no blood, no flying reptile skin. The snake twitched when the bullet hit it, but otherwise it lay motionless.

I found myself standing on the cushion of a nearby chair, the smoking gun in my hand. Doors slammed nearby. I heard querulous voices outside.

The snake still didn't move, didn't writhe in pain, didn't try to slither away. I took another look and realized the snake was made of rubber, one of those sick toys they sell in roadside tourist traps. It wouldn't be doing any slithering, but I had some explaining to do.

The motel's night manager called the cops, naturally, and it didn't take long for an officer to arrive. At first, I thought it was to the young officer's credit that he didn't die laughing on the spot. Then I realized he was too dumb to get the joke, and that I was in for a long haul.

Two hours later, the cop was still saying, "And you don't know who might've left this little surprise for you?"

And I was still saying, "Nope."

Of course, I had a few ideas. It could've been Reasons, getting a little payback for his earlier embarrassment. Plenty of motel guests came and peered through my doorway to see what the commotion was all about, but he wasn't among them. But I didn't think he had enough of a sense of humor to commit a prank. It could've been the women of WOMB, though they shouldn't even know I was still in town. We hadn't been spotted that morning, had we? Or could it have been whoever was in that pickup truck that tried to run me down the night before?

I didn't tell the rookie cop about the near miss with the pickup truck. He seemed to have all he could handle just with this. He took enough notes to make a report the approximate thickness of the Sears catalog. When he finally left, I had the night manager to deal with, the same sourpuss who'd checked me in a couple of days ago. Once I agreed to pay for the ruined mattress, he cheered up a little, and he arranged for a janitor to bring me a new mattress from a vacant room.

It was past midnight by the time everything had been settled, and I fell into the freshly made bed, weary and spent. I went to sleep, my revolver on the nightstand, and dreamed of blue boots full of writhing snakes. I've had better nights.

T W E L V E

■◆■

I awoke to someone pounding on my door. It took me a while to find my jeans and pull them on and rub the sleep off my face and answer. When I yanked the door open, a deputy sheriff stood there, his fist still upraised in mid-knock.

"What?" My voice sounded rough as a gravel pit. The pink-cheeked deputy seemed untroubled by my abruptness.

"You Wilton Mabry?"

"Call me Bubba." My automatic reply.

"You are Mr. Mabry, then?"

"Yes. What is it? I was asleep."

"Sheriff Hernandez wants to see you. Now."

"Can I brush my teeth first?"

The deputy thought that over for a second before nodding. Maybe he'd gotten a whiff of my morning breath and that was the deciding factor. Anyhow, I used the grooming time to wonder what Hernandez wanted.

Could be that he'd heard about the rubber snake incident and wanted to watch me squirm through another retelling. Or maybe he'd gotten wind of my encounter with the rattling pickup truck. The most likely possibility, and the worst one, was that Reasons and I had been spotted going to WOMB the day before and Hernandez had another trespassing charge to slap on us. But it was Sunday morning, a peaceful time for brunching or churching or sleeping late. Would even Hernandez take trespassing so seriously that he'd bust us on Sunday?

My fears seemed to be confirmed when I went outside. The fresh-faced deputy waited, leaning against the hood of his squad car. Reasons already was locked in the backseat.

The deputy held the back door open so I could slide in beside my partner. Then he got behind the wheel and drove us toward the center of town.

Reasons, showing no sign of the blood or sweat or tears he'd displayed when I saw him last, spoke up.

"You know what this is about, Bubba?"

"Not a clue. Maybe this young officer could tell us."

The deputy said nothing.

"Excuse me," Reasons said, louder. "You want to tell us why we're going to see the sheriff?"

"The sheriff will tell you what you need to know when we get there."

My turn. "Does that mean you're under orders not to tell us?"

The deputy eyed me in the rearview mirror.

"That means I don't go shooting my mouth off about the sheriff's business."

Reasons smiled. "Wise beyond his years."

The deputy smiled, too. But he said nothing more. Didn't even ask me about my black eye. Which was just as well, since I was running out of lies.

When we arrived at the courthouse, the deputy marched us inside, straight into Hernandez's office. The sheriff was waiting, all black hair and white teeth, sitting with one leg crossed over the other, using a pencil to pick mud off his cowboy boot. As soon as we were seated in the wooden chairs, he set his foot down and turned to face us.

"Did you boys go out to WOMB yesterday?"

I opened my mouth to lie, but Reasons beat me to the punch. "Yes, sir, we did."

"What time of day?"

"Early yesterday morning. We spoke with a rancher named Valdez. Then we walked into WOMB to look around."

"How long were you there?"

"Not long. Maybe fifteen minutes. Then we came back to town."

"So when did you get back?"

"I don't know exactly. Before noon."

I was flabbergasted. I was certain Hernandez had called us in to lock us up for trespassing, and Reasons hadn't even *tried* to slip out from under the accusation. His moral code for honesty was messing up my case—again.

"You see anything while you were there?"

"Yes, sir. A bunch of the women were swimming at that place where the creek is dammed."

"And Margaret Ogletroop was among them?"

"Yes, sir."

"And?"

Reasons's cheeks flushed at the memory of what he'd seen. I chimed in.

"She and Luna went off into the bushes together for some hanky-panky. Mr. Squeamish here couldn't stand to watch, so we left."

Reasons's face was bright red. He cleared his throat, coughed into his fist. Hernandez's bright smile lit up his face for an instant, then disappeared.

"I thought I told you boys not to go back up there."

"Well, sir, I think what you said was don't go bothering the women of WOMB," I said. "We didn't bother anybody. I don't think they even knew we were there."

As soon as I said that, I realized it was stupid. Somebody must've seen us, or we wouldn't be answering to the sheriff now. But Hernandez nodded, thinking it over.

"And Margaret Ogletroop was fine when you saw her?"

"She seemed to be enjoying herself. Nice Saturday-morning frolic."

He nodded some more, and something clicked in my head.

"Is something wrong with her now?"

"You could say that. She's dead."

"What!" Reasons and I spoke in unison. No need for lying or bluffing here. We were stunned.

"Some of the WOMBsters found her around dawn. They'd missed her during the night but thought she might've decided to go home, or that you boys might've snatched her out of there. At first light, they went looking, and they found her at an altar in the woods. Or at least that's their version."

I managed to stammer out a single word: "Murdered?"

Hernandez nodded. "Unless she could find a way to smash her own head in and then put a pigsticker through her own heart, I'd rule out suicide."

The sheriff flipped over a report on his cluttered desk, fished a couple of Polaroid photos out from under it. He tossed them across his desk and watched us carefully as we each picked one up.

Margaret Ogletroop lay splayed across a large flat rock, one arm draped off onto the ground. Her blond hair was across her face, and she wore a thin cotton sundress soaked with blood, hitched up around her thighs. From her chest, just below her left breast, jutted the deer-horn hilt of a hunting knife. The photo was shot from far enough away that you could see the backdrop to the altar, large slabs of rock set on end, decorated with feathers and bells and seashells.

Reasons found his voice. "She was sacrificed."

"What?"

"Sacrificed on the altar. It makes sense. They've stepped up their pagan worship. First, it was animals, cattle mutilations; now they're sacrificing people."

Hernandez shook his head. "You did talk to old man Valdez, didn't you? We never had any proof WOMB and those cattle mutilations were connected."

Reasons waved the Polaroid at him. "Here's your proof right here."

"That doesn't prove anything. Anybody who wanted to murder her could've staged it at that shrine to make it look like WOMB was responsible."

"Why are you protecting those women?"

Wrong thing to say. Hernandez sat back in his chair, glowering at Reasons.

"I'm not protecting anybody. I've already interviewed Luna, and I've got deputies questioning the other forty or so members of WOMB. If one of them is responsible, we'll find it out."

I interrupted them. "What did Luna say?"

"Well, she was pretty shook up. I figured, even before I talked to you, there was something going on between the two of them. She's really grieving."

Reasons snorted, but the sheriff ignored him.

"She said that altar was Margaret's own personal shrine, her private place. Apparently, a lot of those women have places like that out in the woods, where they go to pray, or whatever it is they do."

"She go there every day?"

Hernandez eyed me. "I asked the same question, but I didn't get a straight answer. They don't watch one another very closely out there. That's why nobody was alarmed when she didn't turn up for supper."

"So they all just went to bed without worrying about her?"

"No. Luna said she was concerned, didn't get much sleep last night. But it's dark in those woods, and they didn't really know where to begin to look for her."

"I think her personal shrine would've been a good place to start."

Hernandez sighed, nodded. "I thought the same thing. But apparently it didn't occur to them until first light."

I hesitated, then pushed ahead.

"Her personal shrine also would be the perfect place to lie in wait for her if you were planning to kill her."

"Exactly my thinking."

"What if it has nothing to do with their religion, as Reasons here keeps saying, but has something to do with Luna? Maybe there's a jealous lover involved."

"We're asking them about that."

"Did you ask Luna?"

"I tried to. Like I said, she was pretty upset. And I guess she's had flings with several of the members, so it makes for a lot of suspects."

"She didn't have a favorite suspect?"

Hernandez grinned.

"Oh yeah. She thinks you two did it."

"What?"

"You were the first suspects to come to mind, anyway. She insisted I round you up right away."

"And you believed her?" Reasons couldn't seem to keep his mouth shut.

"Not necessarily. I would've sent somebody for you, anyway. You *are* suspects. Trespassers, trying to interfere in WOMB's business, after this particular woman." He ticked off our sins on his fingers. "I wouldn't be doing my job if I didn't question you."

I jumped in before Reasons could raise another objection.

"We understand perfectly, Sheriff. But believe me, we want the killer caught as much as you do."

Hernandez pressed his lips together tightly. "I doubt that's possible."

I put the Polaroid of Margaret Ogletroop's body back on Hernandez's desk, and Reasons did likewise.

"Can we go now?" Reasons asked. "You've got everything we know."

"Sure, but you're not planning to leave town right away, are you?"

"I don't know," I said quickly. "We've got to talk to Marcus Ogletroop now, see what he wants done."

"I don't want you to *do* anything," Hernandez said. "Don't stick your noses into my investigation, understand? Let law enforcement handle it. But stay around. I may want to ask you some more questions."

We rose to leave.

"One more thing. Where did you two go after you came back from WOMB yesterday?"

"I stayed in my room all day," Reasons said, "fasting and praying."

"I was in my room, too, for most of the day. Watched a baseball game. Blue Jays won, three to two. Then I went to the Sagebrush Inn for dinner last night, and spent a couple of hours in their bar. When I got back to my room, somebody had pulled a prank on me, left a rubber snake in my bed."

Hernandez grinned despite himself. "I've heard all about that. I've got the report right here."

He tapped a piece of paper on his desk.

"Any idea who did that to you?"

"None. But it scared the bejeezus out of me."

Hernandez chuckled.

"Good thing Margaret Ogletroop wasn't killed with a bullet. Firing your gun after the fact in such a public way would've been a good way to cover up an earlier shooting."

"I'm not that clever."

"Doesn't matter anyway, since no gun was involved in the murder. So, we know where you were last night. What about earlier in the day? You got any witnesses? Anybody who can prove you two were in your motel rooms?"

After a long, uncomfortable silence, we both shook our heads.

Hernandez said, "Hmm," and made a note on a piece of paper with his pencil. The way I felt, standing there with my crumbling alibi, he might as well have written "Guilty."

"Okay," he said, "I'll be in touch. Have a nice day."

T H I R T E E N
■ ◆ ■

Reasons and I reeled outside, blinking and squinting in the bright sunshine. Everything I'd assumed about WOMB had just been turned upside down. Despite their spears and arrows and outrageous behavior, I'd presumed the WOMBsters were a peaceful bunch, reveling in their bucolic existence. Men make all the wars, right? Without men around, wouldn't women get along?

Of course, there had been some men around—us. Maybe Margaret became a liability once Reasons and I showed up. Maybe someone didn't want that much attention focused on WOMB. But if they had something to hide up there, it had remained hidden. We certainly hadn't stumbled across it.

Reasons seemed as dazed as I was. We wandered along a sidewalk by the parking lot, saying nothing, both lost in our thoughts. A muscle in his cheek twitched from keeping his jaw clamped shut. Sure, now he shuts up, I thought. In the sheriff's office, he'd had diarrhea of the mouth, running off our itinerary from the day before. I felt like pinching him.

A thick-bodied cottonwood leaned over an old wooden bench

at the street corner, and Reasons sat down in the shade. I sat beside him. We stared out at the passing cars, each waiting for the other to speak.

"That poor girl," he said finally.

"Yeah. She still had a lot of living ahead of her."

Reasons shook his head slightly.

"It's too late for that," he said. "I was thinking about her soul. If she turned her back on God for those pagan ways, then she died in sin. I won't be seeing her in heaven."

Here we go again. I scooted away from him on the bench, getting a splinter in my butt in the process.

"There's a lesson in this for you, Bubba. Don't turn your back on God. You never know when death might be waiting for you."

There's a lesson here all right, I thought. I need to get away from Purvis Reasons before he drives me crazy. That seemed possible now. With Margaret Ogletroop dead, we had no case to pursue together. He could go his way and I could go mine. I just hoped the Ogletroops wouldn't demand their thousand bucks back.

I sat in silence, formulating arguments about retainers and expenses, as a maroon Range Rover pulled up to the curb in front of us. Marcus Ogletroop sat behind the wheel, scowling at us.

The window rolled down with a hum. Reasons and I got to our feet slowly, no doubt looking whipped. But Ogletroop showed no mercy.

"Well, if it isn't our crack investigators. I figured you two would mess things up, but I never expected Margaret to end up dead."

Up close, Ogletroop's eyes looked red and bleary. It figured that someone of his temperament would take his mourning out on his subordinates. I kept my mouth shut.

"We just heard about it from the sheriff," Reasons said. "I'm sorry for your loss."

"You're sorry? You should be sorry." He adopted a whiny

tone. " 'We can get her out of WOMB, Mr. Ogletroop. No problem, Mr. Ogletroop.' What crap. At least when she was at WOMB, Margaret was still alive. Now where is she?"

"We can only hope she's in heaven."

I winced. Ogletroop's face darkened until I thought blood would spurt out of his head like the mercury in an overheated thermometer.

"You damned fool." The words came quick and low. "I tried to tell my grandmother that you were trouble, with all your religious claptrap, but she wouldn't listen."

So far, Reasons was taking the brunt of this. That was fine by me.

"And you, Mabry. I thought you had some street savvy, some experience. But you're just as much a fuckup as he is."

I'd had enough. I grabbed the door of the Range Rover with both hands and leaned in through the window.

"Watch it, Marcus. You're pushing too hard. I know you're upset about your sister, but we didn't kill her. We didn't do anything you weren't paying us to do. So don't try to blame us now."

Ogletroop leaned away from me. His mouth curved downward into a sneer, and I expected him to say more, but something in my expression must've cowed him, because he clammed up and looked away. He sneaked a peek at me to see if I was still glaring at him, found that I was, then studied the steering wheel some more.

"I'm sorry," he said finally. "I'm so wiped out. They called me this morning, told me to fly up here and claim Margaret's body. I just couldn't believe it."

I felt myself softening.

"I know, I know. We're stunned, too. Why don't you give us a lift back to the motel, and we'll talk it over."

He nodded, and we climbed into the Range Rover.

Ogletroop was too distracted to drive, weaving over the center line, blinking tears away. He blew through a red light, nearly clipped a streetlight as he swung into the Holiday Inn's parking lot. I looked over my shoulder at Reasons, who'd taken the backseat. His lips moved in silent prayer.

Ogletroop slammed to a stop in front of my room. I didn't know how he knew which room I was staying in, but I didn't ask. Mundane questions didn't seem to fit right now, with the man's sister laid out on a slab somewhere.

Reasons and I bailed out of the Range Rover, and he looked pleased to have survived the ride. Ogletroop sat behind the wheel, the engine still running.

"Aren't you coming in?"

"I've got to go see the sheriff. Identify Margaret's body."

"There's no hurry," I said, thinking, She's not going anywhere. "Let's talk first."

He blinked and sighed, shut off the engine.

My room still reeked of gunpowder from the snake shooting. The maid hadn't been by while I was gone, and the bedclothes were wadded and twisted. I opened the curtains to let in some light, and left the door standing open to let out the odor. Reasons and Ogletroop took the two chairs by the window; I sat on the unmade bed.

Ogletroop took a deep, shuddering breath. "All right, tell me what you know."

Reasons and I looked at each other, each waiting for the other to begin. I could see in his eyes that Reasons didn't want to take the lead, that he was afraid of another outburst from Ogletroop. I plunged ahead.

"Yesterday morning, as per your instructions, we went back up to WOMB," I began. "We found a way to get on their property from the neighboring ranch without being spotted. Then we hiked down to where a bunch of the women were skinny-dipping.

102

"Your sister was there. She was with the woman who runs the place, Luna. They, um, they clearly were more than just friends. Know what I mean?"

Ogletroop went wide-eyed for a second, then got hold of himself, nodded.

"We left after a little while and came back to town." I glanced over at Reasons, but he wouldn't look at me. I spared him, not telling Ogletroop why we'd left so abruptly.

"Nothing else happened until this morning when Sheriff Hernandez sent someone to fetch us. That's when we found out Margaret had been killed."

"What did you tell the sheriff?"

"Just what I've told you. There's really nothing more to tell."

There was more: the rattling pickup truck, the rubber rattler, the fact that I was going to kill Reasons if he wasn't out of my life soon. But I figured Ogletroop didn't need to hear all that. The man had just lost his sister.

We all sat in silence for a minute. Ogletroop cleared his throat, spoke hesitatingly. "So that's all you had accomplished so far?"

"We were being careful," I said quickly. "We didn't know we needed to be in a hurry. If we'd known Margaret was in danger, I guess we could've stormed the place and gotten her out in time. But who knew? Your last instruction to us was to stay after it without getting arrested. That meant caution and taking it slow."

Ogletroop nodded.

"My grandmother said the same thing this morning."

"How is she doing?"

"Oh, she's handling it all right, I guess. I was afraid her heart would just give out when she heard the news. But she took it like a man."

He realized what he'd just said, gave a halfhearted chuckle.

"You'd have to know my grandmother better to appreciate that. She'd take it as a compliment."

I nodded in agreement. I would've guessed as much. The old woman's generation didn't seem to have as many hang-ups about men as women do now. Men weren't automatically the bumbling bad guys. And she'd been running things so long that she was beyond gender. She was commander in chief.

"What did she say about us?" I felt ridiculous asking the question. It sounded like the kind of thing a schoolboy would ask about a girl he had a crush on: Did she say anything about me? Did my name come up? But staying in the Goddess's good graces was closely linked to keeping her thousand bucks.

Ogletroop stared out the window at the mountains, an expression of pain on his face.

"She seems to have taken a shine to you, Mabry," he said. "She said she wanted you to stay on the case, try to find out who killed Margaret."

I managed not to beam.

Reasons said, "What about me?"

Ogletroop turned his head to face Reasons, and his eyebrows creased toward each other.

"Your services will no longer be needed," he said icily. "Why would we need a deprogrammer when the person to be deprogrammed is dead?"

"But I know about cults. I'm an expert."

Ogletroop slowly shook his head.

"If Mabry wants you to stay on to help him, he can pay you. We're done with you."

"This isn't about the money," Reasons said. "I want those women brought to justice. They have to be stopped before someone else dies. Bubba, you'll need my help, right?"

He looked desperate, and I felt bad for him, sure, but I wasn't about to keep him around another second longer than necessary. He'd nearly driven me crazy over the past few days, had me thinking all the time about God and sin and death. Who needed it? But I wasn't about to hash that out in front of Ogletroop.

"We'll talk about it later," I said, tilting my head toward the grieving brother so he'd get my drift.

"I can't leave Taos, anyway," he said. "The sheriff wants us to stay around. I might as well help."

"Later."

He nodded and sat back in his chair. Ogletroop turned his attention back to me.

"What do you propose to do?"

"I don't rightly know, to tell you the truth. I'm out of my element here. I don't know anybody in Taos except the sheriff, and I'd rather not spend any more time in his office. If this was Albuquerque, I could hit the streets, talk to my sources, come up with some clues. Here, I'm sort of stuck.

"The most likely suspects are up at WOMB. I can try to go up there and interview some of them, I guess, but I don't think they're going to talk to me. They think Reasons and I killed Margaret. Or at least that's what Luna told the sheriff. Maybe I'll go back up there and snoop around. We have a good way of sneaking onto their ranch now. . . ."

Ogletroop shook his head to shush me.

"I'm sorry I asked. I don't want to know what you're going to try. I don't even know why my grandmother would want you to stay with it. Just do the best you can."

He sighed and got to his feet.

"I've got to go see the sheriff. I'm not looking forward to this, seeing Margaret that way."

I stood up, too.

"I could do it for you." The words were out of my mouth before I thought about them. I'm not crazy about seeing corpses.

But at least it was something I could do for the family, something that might ingratiate me with Marcus.

"No," he said, "I'll do it. It's my responsibility. I should take it like a man."

F O U R T E E N

■ ◆ ■

Ogletroop had been gone maybe thirty seconds when we heard a tremendous boom outside. For an instant, I thought he'd plowed the Range Rover into the building, but the boom lasted too long to be an impact. It was thunder.

I stood up, looked out the window. To the east, the direction I could see, the sky was still sunny and blue. But there was some change in the light—a hint of shadow—that told me a thunderhead was rolling in from the west.

Summer is lightning season in New Mexico. Rising temperatures push all the clouds together into huge nimbus generators. The wind picks up; the clouds race across the sky; lightning dances near the ground. Occasionally, it even rains. Out here, the ranchers say a six-inch rain is one drop every six inches. Sometimes, the rain will come down in buckets, but it's extremely localized. I've seen it pouring on one side of a street and bone-dry on the other. Like a lot of New Mexicans, I don't even own an umbrella. If it starts raining, you just find shelter and wait it out. It won't take long.

As they say out in these parts, Lightning does the work; thunder takes the credit. The thunder can be awesome, mind-numbing, but the lightning is the show. Not that wimpy heat lightning like they get back east. We're talking jagged streaks of lightning, blasting the ground, setting forest fires. New Mexico has more lightning deaths per capita than anywhere in the country. But it's never scared me. I love fireworks.

The thunder rumbled again, closer. I itched to get out of the close motel room and into the wind-whipped air. But I had something to settle first.

Reasons still sat in the chair, watching my every move with eager puppy-dog eyes. Getting rid of him wasn't going to be easy.

One problem with growing up southern is that it makes you too damned polite. Sometimes, you need to be abrupt, rude even. It's the only thing some people understand. But southerners can't bring themselves to come right out and say something. We have to sidle up to an unpleasant subject, slather it with molasses, present it as something tasty.

What I wanted to say to Reasons was something like, Get out, and don't let the door hit you in the ass as you go. What I actually said was, "Looks like rain."

"Yes." He still watched me, waiting.

"Marcus seems to be having a hard time handling this."

"He's had a grave loss."

"Too bad about Margaret. Sure turned out to be an interesting case, though."

"It's not over yet," he said.

"Well, no, it's not. Not exactly. But we won't be doing any kidnapping. She's gone."

"You have any idea who did it?"

"Not really. I kind of like the notion that it might've been a woman who was jealous about her relationship with Luna. But

I'll be damned if I can figure how to prove that. It's not like they're going to sit still for quizzing."

He nodded, looked thoughtful. Looked, in fact, like he had an idea.

"Don't discount the religious aspect," he said. "I still think it could be a ritual murder."

I shook my head.

"They knew we were up there looking for Margaret," I said. "The sheriff was involved. That would be the absolute wrong time to sacrifice her. Why not pick somebody else for that, someone more anonymous? And, once Margaret was dead, why report it to the sheriff?"

He leaned back in his chair and sighed.

"I'm talking religion here, Bubba. We can't expect it always to be logical. Look at history. Religious fanatics have been killing people forever. Still are. The Inquisition. The Salem witch trials. The jihad in the Middle East. Once people are convinced God—or the goddess, or Allah, or whoever—is on their side, they're likely to do anything."

As he talked, I saw him as I had yesterday—squatting over the toilet, his teeth clenched and eyes streaming as he whacked himself with that little whip, purging evil thoughts. And now he's talking about fanatics. He should know, I thought; he should know.

"I've witnessed some of these pagan rituals," he said. "They're frenzied affairs. Dancing around bonfires, thumping drums, sometimes drugs or sex right out in the open. In a situation like that, things can get out of hand. Suddenly, somebody gets a 'vision' that the goddess wants Margaret dead; it's not such a great leap."

"Sounds to me like you're saying a big party turns to murder. It doesn't seem likely."

"It's been known to happen."

The thunder boomed again, right overhead, and I looked out the window, waiting for rain. The whole day was cast into shadow by the thunderheads.

There was something to what he said, but I couldn't seem to get a grip on it. The WOMBsters, despite the way they'd treated us, seemed more like peaceful, goofy New Agers than the ribald witches he was making them out to be. I couldn't imagine them getting so worked up that they'd off one of their own in a public sacrifice. If they were going to sacrifice a person, wouldn't it have been a man? Why not Reasons or me? They had us caught, and no one knew we were there. It would've been the perfect opportunity.

No, if Margaret Ogletroop's death was all about religion, then it was an outsider, someone who saw himself as God's crusader, saving the WOMBsters from their own abhorrent beliefs. Someone like Reasons.

I turned, studied him. The fire burned behind his eyes. He looked like he was trying not to smile. I opened my mouth to speak, but the thunder rolled, drowning out whatever I might've said.

His alibi was lamer than mine. In his room all day, fasting and praying. Nobody there to vouch for him. If a man is wacky enough about God to flog himself over one peek at some flesh, how much of a jump would it be for him to go out to WOMB and save Margaret from sin by killing her?

I could picture him at that altar, kneeling over her, mumbling prayers. The knife is raised, brought down sharply, and Margaret's a goner. Of course, I'd never seen a knife in Reasons's possession. As far as I knew, he didn't even have access to a car at the moment; how would he have gone out there? But he could've rented another one, and that was easy enough to check out.

He sat there, looking smug, as if he could see my wheels turning, knew what I was thinking. If he'd done it, why hadn't he run? Maybe he thought he'd pulled off the perfect crime and he was willing to ride it out. Maybe he thought God was protecting him.

Thunder cracked sharply. I turned and looked out the window as the first fat raindrops dotted the parking lot.

"You know," he said behind me, "when I was a child, I was afraid of thunder. My mother used to soothe me by telling me it was the sound of angels bowling."

"Bowling?"

"Mm-hmm. One of my first notions about religion was angels in their white robes and multicolored shoes, rolling their bowling balls, trying for a strike."

Lightning streaked the sky right in front of me. It looked as if it had hit the ground less than a mile away. The thunder crashed immediately, and the rain suddenly sped up, pouring now, torrential.

The window was sheltered by an awning, so the rain couldn't blow in. I cracked it open, sniffed the air. Desert rain creates a distinctive fragrance, a mix of dust and water and sagebrush and ionized air. It's one of the best scents I know.

"It's really coming down out there now, isn't it?" Reasons said, joining me at the window.

"It's a frog-strangler all right, but it won't last long."

We watched the rain. I sighed, knowing what I had to say next. I could barely stand the thought of spending any more time around Purvis Reasons, but I needed to keep him nearby. He was a suspect, a pretty damned good one at that. Hell, at this point, *everyone* was a suspect. The only person I could be sure hadn't killed Margaret was me, and that's only because I'd been watching myself the whole time. Now I needed to watch Reasons.

I waited while the thunder rumbled again, then turned to him, ready to say my piece before the next boomer.

"Look, I want you to stay on the case with me, at least temporarily." He beamed. "But you've got to lay off all the God talk, okay? It's making me crazy."

The smile eased off his face, but he propped it up again.

"I'll do my best," he said. He said something more, but it was drowned out by thunder.

When the rumble stopped, I started to ask him to repeat himself, but I heard a steady knocking. Reasons heard it, too. We stared at each other, eyebrows raised. I wondered if lightning had hit the building, whether the knocking was something structural giving way. It continued, persistent, getting louder.

"Somebody's at the door," he said.

"Oh."

I flung open the door. There, soaked through, her wet hair hanging in her face, stood Felicia.

"Got a towel?"

"Hi. Uh, sure. Come in."

I hurried into the bathroom for a clean towel, leaving her to introduce herself to Reasons.

I handed Felicia the towel and she sponged at her hair with it. She took off her rain-spattered glasses and handed them to me. I hustled after some Kleenex to clean them.

"Goddamn, that rain's cold."

I turned in time to see Reasons stiffen at her choice of words.

"It's the altitude," I said quickly. "We're higher than a mile here. The rain doesn't have time to warm up on its way to the ground."

She pursed her lips at me, as if to say she knew that already. But her expression softened when I handed her the dry eyeglasses. She clamped them on her face and looked around the room.

Her white blouse was so soaked that I could see her bra beneath it. It looked as if you could wring a gallon of water from her blue jeans.

"What are you doing here?"

"What's the matter? Aren't you glad to see me?"

"Sure, I—"

"You don't act like it."

"Sorry." I leaned over, gave her a peck on the lips. It embarrassed me to do it in front of Reasons (public displays of affection being definitely prohibited by a southern upbringing), but I had no choice. The truth was, I would've liked to run Reasons off and get Felicia out of her wet things, but he didn't seem to be going anywhere.

"So," I said, "what *are* you doing here?"

"I'm here to investigate Margaret Ogletroop's murder. We heard about it at the paper this morning, and I persuaded my editors to send me to cover it."

I could just imagine how that persuasion session must've gone. Once Felicia decides she wants something, it's best just to get out of the way.

"I had to drop your name to convince them," she said, trying not to smile. "I told them you were already up here doing an investigation and I could team up with you."

She knows I hate that. It's hard to keep a low profile when she tosses my name around her newsroom. Of course, it doesn't happen often. Usually, she's not so proud of our relationship that she trumpets about it. But when a story is involved, I've found, Felicia will do or say just about anything to land it.

"You know I prefer to work alone," I said.

She tilted her head toward Reasons, as if to say, What about him?

"That was different. Purvis here was sort of foisted upon me. And now, like it or not, we're a team."

Reasons smiled.

"God brought us together," he said.

"Now cut that out! I told you I've heard enough of that."

He nodded, still smiling, his hands clasped before him as if he was about to say grace.

Felicia rolled her eyes. "You know, Bubba, for someone who doesn't seem to believe in God, you sure get mixed up with a lot of religious nuts."

The smile disappeared from Reasons's face. Apparently, "nut" was the one disparagement that would get to him. Leave it to Felicia to hit on it within two minutes of meeting him.

Naturally, she took no notice of his sudden scowl. She rarely notices mine, either.

"Okay, tell me what's been going on up here."

"Wouldn't you rather get into some dry clothes first?"

She looked down at her sopping garments as if she hadn't noticed until now that she was drenched.

"Yeah, I guess so. That's a good idea."

"Are your clothes out in your car?"

"Yeah, so are my cameras. I didn't want everything to get soaked while I was finding your room."

"How did you know where it was?"

"I ran in and asked at the lobby. Then I pulled my car around here."

"You could've waited a few minutes. It looks like it's letting up out there already."

"Hey, I've got a deadline. Neither rain nor snow. . ."

"Yeah, yeah, I know. But you've got lots of time. Why don't you change clothes? Then we'll go get something to eat."

"I guess I should check in, get a room, unload my stuff."

"You could stay here with me. The Ogletroops already are paying for this room."

"Nah. Let 'em pay for another one. I'll be working late into the night. I don't want to bother you."

"No bother."

Felicia glanced over at Reasons, shook her head. "Nah. I'll get my own room."

Reasons asked me questions about Felicia while she was gone—how long we'd known each other, if we could trust her, whether it would be a problem having the newspapers involved. I wanted to turn the conversation, get back to his possible motives and size up whether he could be the killer. But he was a one-track sort of guy. It was like turning a freight train.

He seemed delighted to be included in the late lunch with Felicia, practically wagging his tail behind him.

I filled Felicia in on everything that had happened since I'd arrived in Taos. It was much like the account I'd given Ogletroop and the sheriff, except I didn't leave anything out, including the rattling pickup truck that had nearly run me down. Reasons occasionally filled in anything I missed, but he didn't have a lot to say. He seemed nervous around Felicia, as if every time he opened his face, he was risking a put-down. Not too far from wrong.

Felicia, taking notes with her right hand and shoveling food with her left, got me to describe in detail the Polaroid photos of the crime scene. The description did nothing to diminish her appetite. Reporters—the only people, besides maybe cops, who sit around and talk about gore as a way of amusing themselves. Reporters are the only folks you'll ever hear talking about a "great" plane crash.

By the time we were done, I was exhausted. It was as if retelling all the events was akin to living through them again. My knee ached where I'd banged it on the street, and I could practically feel Judah nudging me along with her spear.

"So," Felicia said when it was clear I'd run out of gas, "what are you going to do now?"

"I honestly don't know. We can't infiltrate WOMB, and it's not likely they'll talk to Reasons and me. We're not supposed to go up there, anyway. I imagine the sheriff's keeping an eye on us."

I wasn't about to say I was keeping an eye on Reasons, waiting for some sign he was guilty. Not with him sitting right there. I may be gullible and clumsy, but I'm not stupid.

"What about you?" I asked. "What are you going to do?"

Felicia squinted at me through her cigarette smoke.

"Well, it doesn't sound like I'm going to hang out with you guys. You're getting nowhere fast."

What could I say? When you're right, you're right.

"I've got a story to write," she said. "I'm going to interview the sheriff, see if I can get anything else out of him. Then I'll probably go back to my room and write it up."

When she's on the road, Felicia uses a laptop computer with a built-in modem to file her stories. She hates the machine, and I'm sure it feels the same way about her. She spills ashes in the keyboard and throws the computer's carrying case around like it's a well-padded handbag. The newspaper regularly replaces the computer with a new model, but so far nobody's thought of replacing the abusive user.

"Okay," I said. "Give us a call when you're done. Maybe we'll go to dinner, and you can fill us in on what you get."

"Maybe so," she said as she got up from the table. "But it'll probably be late. This is a big story, one the Goddess will be watching closely. I've got to give it my best."

She hurried out of the café, leaving me holding the check. Reasons blinked a few times, watching her go.

"What did she mean, the goddess would be watching her?"

"It's a long story."

F I F T E E N

■ ◆ ■

I slept later than I'd intended the next morning. I'd stayed up late, making sure Reasons was bedded down for the night before turning in myself. I'd knocked on Felicia's door after she missed dinner, but nobody was home. I figured she was working late, probably giving Sheriff Hernandez the third degree. I took pleasure in the idea that it was his turn to be grilled. Felicia was just the woman to do it.

Though I wouldn't have admitted it, I was glad Felicia was on the scene. I needed an ally, someone I could brainstorm with, and she was good at that. Her ideas are always more outlandish and bolder than my own. Sometimes, they're just what I need to spur me into action. I found myself whistling while I showered up and dressed.

I knocked on her door again. Still no answer. Her Toyota wasn't in the parking lot.

I ambled down to the lobby, thinking maybe she'd left me a message about where she'd gone. A bright-eyed young blonde behind the counter was only too happy to check, and, sure enough, there was a note from Felicia, scrawled on a piece of paper ripped out of her reporter's notebook. The blonde eyed my shiner, and I smiled at her as she handed over the note. I nearly fell over backward when I read it:

Bubba,

Turned up very little talking to that idiot sheriff.
Decided to go up to WOMB, maybe sign up as a
member. Don't come up there. You'll blow my cover.
I'll be in touch.

Felicia

"Jesus Christ!"

"Bad news?" The blonde behind the counter had watched me read the message.

"The worst."

"Sorry." She tossed her head. "Anything the motel can do?"

"Not unless the staff wants to form a posse."

"Huh?"

I shook her off and hurried out of the lobby. What could Felicia be thinking? There was a good chance a murderer was loose in WOMB, and she just waltzes in there, asks to join up. If they found out she was a reporter, it could be the last bad decision Felicia ever made.

I jogged to Reasons's room, banged on the door until he opened up.

"Good morning."

"Not so far." I handed him the note.

He read it, shaking his head the whole time.

"This is bad. This is very bad."

"I know. It's just like her to run off and do something like this without checking with me."

"She seems to be a very headstrong woman."

"That's the understatement of the year."

He waved the note at me.

"What should we do about this?"

"Get your shit together. We're going to WOMB."

"But this says—"

"I know what it says. She doesn't know what she's getting herself into. We've got to do something."

"But we can't just storm in there—"

"Look, stop flapping your jaws and get your binoculars and
stuff. We'll go up there the way we did the other day, sneak
around, see if we can spot her."

We met at my car a few minutes later and took off for WOMB.

I stopped at the entrance to WOMB, just long enough for Reasons to leap out and peer up the driveway toward the settlement.

"I saw her car," he said breathlessly when he rejoined me in
the Chevy. "Brown Toyota, right? It's parked in a little clearing
just up the way, next to a van with a license plate that says
BROOM."

I drove on. Nobody seemed to be home at the Valdez place.
We let ourselves through the gate and followed the rutted road
up onto the ridge. We had to wait several minutes before a
couple of dim-witted Herefords finished their chewing and ambled out of the way. I was nervous as a porcupine in a balloon
factory, but I didn't honk or yell. I'd promised the old rancher I
wouldn't spook his herd.

Before we got out of the car, I gave Reasons another lecture.

"Look, they're going to be on guard because of Margaret's
murder. We'll have to be very careful. Keep your eyes peeled. If
Felicia has convinced them she's a potential new member, then
spotting us might tip them off to her."

He nodded, a grim set to his mouth.

"If she hasn't convinced them, then we might have to bust into the place and get her out. Are you ready to do such a thing?"

"God will show us the way."

"Stop that! I'm not asking about God. I'm asking about you. Can I count on you?"

"I'm your humble servant."

I sighed loudly, and popped open the car door. "Let's go."

We walked down the trail alongside the granite outcrop, slowly and quietly. Inside, all my personal alarms clanged. I was going back to WOMB against all my better judgment. The WOMBsters thought we killed Margaret, so, if we were caught, it might be all over for us. Sheriff Hernandez had warned us not to come out here again, so he'd be no help. And, my number-one suspect in Margaret's murder was my backup man. Sheesh.

No one was swimming at the dammed-up pool. We crept around it, keeping to the underbrush.

After about fifty yards on our hands and knees, we came upon a little clearing dominated by a stone altar. I could see at a glance it was the altar in the Polaroids the sheriff had shown us. Dried blood still darkened the central slab. The dirt around it was covered by footprints going every which way, heavy boots from the cops, smaller, lighter prints from the women of WOMB.

"Guess the rain didn't get up here yesterday," I whispered to Reasons.

He looked puzzled, then followed my finger when I pointed to the altar. It dawned on him where we were, and he immediately began praying, his lips moving, his eyes half-shut. I sighed, looked to heaven for some relief.

I wanted to study the altar up close, check it for clues, but I didn't want to be caught standing in the clearing. We skirted the opening in the trees, crept toward the ranch house and the other buildings.

As we got close, we moved up the wooded hillside so we could look down into the compound. The place was shut up tight, nobody strolling around outside, no sign of any guards. I figured they were stationed down by the road to turn away TV crews or whoever showed up.

Reasons and I found a pretty good spot to watch from, a cluster of lichen-furred boulders with young pines jutting up through them. We settled down into the shade ten feet apart, put our binoculars to our eyes, and didn't move again for the next few hours.

There wasn't much to see. Maybe the WOMBsters were in mourning, or maybe the blazing sun was just keeping them indoors where it was cool. But there was none of the activity we'd spotted before. As the hours passed, I became convinced they were all inside working on Felicia, trying to wash my sweetie's brain. Reasons, when he finally crawled over to me, had the same speculations.

"If they're indoctrinating her," he whispered, "they're probably all in the same room, chanting or praying or whatever they do. Maybe that's why we see no one."

"How long will that take?"

"Depends."

"On what?"

"On how receptive she is, or how well she can persuade them that she's buying the program. Is she a believer? Is her faith strong?"

"About all Felicia believes in is the next story she gets in the paper."

Reasons chewed on that for a moment.

"Actually, that might be good," he said. "If she doesn't have a lot of convictions to overcome, she can probably fake the new beliefs better. Does she have a strong mind?"

"The strongest."

"Good. She'll need it."

"What do you think they're doing to her?"

"Persuading her the goddess is the right route. Teaching her to hate men."

Ouch. I didn't like the sound of that.

Reasons offered me a drink from the canteen.

"This water isn't going to last much longer," he said.

"That's okay. I think we're going to get all the water we need pretty soon."

I pointed to the west, where I'd noticed storm clouds building in the distance.

"Think that's headed this way?"

"Yeah."

"And we'll just sit out here in it?"

"I don't see how we've got a lot of choice."

He nodded, thinking it over. Then he crawled back to his vantage point and returned to watching WOMB.

It wasn't long before the fast-moving clouds were directly overhead. A pile of boulders isn't the best place to sit during a lightning storm, but I wasn't giving up our good lookout post. As the first drops fell, Reasons and I crowded together under the little pines, clinging to their trunks like they were parasols.

The rain came cold and fast but lasted only a few minutes. I still had a few dry places on my clothes when it stopped. Maybe four drops fell into our open canteen.

The clouds broke apart over Wheeler Peak and rays of sun fell down onto WOMB. Steam soon rose from our clothes. We sat there, steaming, waiting for something, anything, to happen.

I'll give Reasons credit for this much: He never once complained. He didn't have much of a stake in watching for Felicia, but he put himself to the task as stalwartly as if she were his sister. As the day crept past, I found myself wondering whether I was full of shit when I considered him a suspect. Would someone who'd committed murder be willing to sit on a pile of rocks all day, through heat and rain, with somebody who suspected him? If the situation was reversed, I would've fidgeted all day, wanting to keep as far away from the scene of the crime as possible. Reasons just prayed and stayed.

S I X T E E N

■ ◆ ■

Nightfall was approaching, and I was about ready to give it up, when we finally spotted some movement at WOMB. Reasons hissed at me and pointed to the ranch house.

Through the binoculars, I watched a towering black woman with muscles like a pole-vaulter step down from the porch. She carried what I first thought to be a large hatbox, then recognized as a drum. She strode to the dusty clearing in the center of the compound, squatted over the drum, and began beating out a rhythm with her hands. The drumbeats echoed around the bowl-shaped ranch. I could feel them reverberate in my chest.

Other women spilled out of the house, silent and serious, arranging themselves in a ring around the clearing. I scanned their faces, looking for Felicia. Instead, I spotted jumbo Judah; approaching the center of the circle, her big arms wrapped around maybe twenty pounds of dry sticks. She dropped them in the center of the circle, then disappeared around the side of the house. She returned with an armload of logs, threw them on the pile, then stooped and lit the whole thing. Soon, she had a major bonfire going, throwing flickering orange light onto the faces of the others. Then she joined the circle. They all clasped hands and began to chant. We couldn't understand the words from where we sat. It reached us as a high-pitched drone, a sound like a buzz saw.

The volume climbed a notch as Luna and Felicia appeared on the porch. They held hands, which put a lump in my throat. Luna was dressed as before in skirt and loose blouse; Felicia wore jeans and a white tunic trimmed with turquoise ribbons around the edges. It was hard to tell at this distance, but Felicia didn't look scared, didn't seem ready to bolt. Luna led her to the bonfire, whispered something in her ear, and Felicia knelt on the ground, perilously close to the fire.

It was all I could do to sit still. Felicia looked virginal and sacrificial in that white blouse, and she was in the perfect position for the kind of bludgeoning that had killed Margaret Ogletroop. If they'd found her out somehow, wouldn't she be the perfect human sacrifice? Wouldn't you get extra points for offering up a reporter?

Felicia looked unworried. If anything, she seemed to be smiling a little. Hard to tell with her head bowed over like that. Why would she be smiling? Maybe she *wanted* to join WOMB. What if they'd succeeded in brainwashing her? What if Felicia now hated men, loved Luna, worshiped the goddess? How would I ever get her back?

Reasons crawled over beside me, rested his hand on my arm. I didn't take the binoculars away from my eyes.

"What?"

"I just wanted to comfort you. I don't want you to do anything foolish." He spoke in a whisper. I didn't look at him.

"Why would I do that?"

"It looks like they're inducting her, that her plan is working. We can't afford to make any sudden moves."

I took the glasses away from my eyes, glanced over at Reasons. It was dark under the spindly pines, but I could still see the concern in his eyes, the worry wrinkling his forehead.

"Did you think I was about to do something stupid?"

"It's hard to do nothing at a time like this. But anything we could do, I'm afraid, would be something stupid."

I swallowed that, nodded.

"As long as they don't hurt her," I said, "I'll sit here and watch. If it looks like another sacrifice is in the works, we'll see how fast you can follow me through these trees."

"Fair enough."

We both put binoculars back to our eyes, watched the scene below.

Luna had what looked like a whisk broom in her hands. She shouted above the chanting, "The purification begins!"

Luna stuck the broom into the fire, where it caught, smoldering, spewing smoke. She approached Felicia with the hot stick, and I tensed, ready to bolt down the hillside.

"It's okay," Reasons whispered beside me. "It's a sage stick. Indians use the smoke in their ceremonies."

Luna circled Felicia three times with the smoking stick, walking in a half crouch. She seemed to be talking to her in low tones. I wished we were close enough to hear. As near as I could tell, Felicia didn't flinch, didn't choke on the smoke. Of course, as many cigarettes as she inhales every day, it probably seemed like fresh air to her.

Luna spun away from Felicia in little dancing steps, then made for the circle of women, waving the smoking wand at each of them. Some of them unclasped hands to fan the smoke toward their faces, inhaling deeply.

The drummer stepped up the rhythm as Luna made her way around the circle. The drumming had been slow and methodical as a heartbeat, but now it was more frantic, more primal.

Women twitched at the sound of it, chanting harder, louder, until we could make out the words.

"Bring us blessings, without men. Bring us blessings, without men. . . ."

I wondered whether Reasons and I squatting in the woods would mess up their blessing, whether the initiation wouldn't take if male pheromones drifted in the air nearby. Maybe Felicia would sense us up here and it would keep her from being swept up by the fervor of WOMB.

When Luna completed the circle, the chanting and drumming abruptly stopped, leaving a silent hole in the night. Luna stood behind Felicia, her head thrown back to the sky. Suddenly, the witch pulled from the waistband of her skirt a long pointed object, a knife. I squinted through the binoculars, saw that the knife was made of chipped flint, long and gnarly. I watched helplessly as Luna raised the knife over her head, ready to bring it down between Felicia's shoulder blades.

Luna pointed the knife toward the sky, where the first stars glowed.

"Hail Guardian of the celestial world!" she shrieked. Felicia flinched at the sudden noise behind her, but she didn't jump up and run. She didn't even turn her head to look at Luna.

"Hail the fertile goddess!" Luna shouted.

"Hail the Earth that is her child.

"Hail the sky, the stars.

"Hail the goddess!

"Bring us blessings, without men!"

Luna pointed the long knife directly at Reasons and me, or at least in the direction of the boulders where we cowered.

"Hail the south! Powers of fire! Bathe us in your purity and warmth."

She pointed the knife to the sky, turned a quarter of the way around the circle, and pointed it toward where Judah stood.

127

"Hail the west! Powers of water! Wash us clean with the waters of her living womb!"

Reasons turned toward me, wrinkled his nose. I put my finger to my lips, then the binoculars back to my eyes.

"Hail the north! Powers of earth! Cornerstone of all life. Send us your strength!"

She turned again, pointed past Felicia.

"Hail the east! Powers of air! Smoke and sunlight! Fill us with her breath!"

Luna followed her pointed knife to the edge of the circle, where two women parted to let her pass. She stooped and dragged the knife in the dust, walking backward as she drew a line around all the women.

When the circle was finished, she ducked under the clutched hands of the chanting women and straightened, a little red in the face from the effort. She walked to the middle of the circle.

"The circle is cast. We are beyond time, between worlds. The fire is lit. The ritual is begun."

Luna approached Felicia, who still knelt by the fire. Luna pulled something from the pocket of her skirt, a heavy necklace, and draped it over Felicia's head, around her neck. She placed her hand on top of Felicia's head like a faith healer and shouted, her head pitched back to launch the words toward the sky.

"Bless this initiate! May her feet walk on the sky. May her hands always do thy bidding."

She took Felicia's hands, pulled her to her feet. Holding Felicia's hand, she turned slowly, turning Felicia with her, facing all the women around the circle.

"If that which you seek isn't found within yourself, you will never find it without."

Luna put her arm around Felicia's shoulders, kissed her on the cheek. I flinched.

"Women of WOMB," she shouted, "I present our newest sister, Felicia."

The women erupted in applause and cheers. The drummer resumed whaling away on the drum skins. The women broke into a wild dance to the rhythm, circling the fire. Luna pulled Felicia close, hugged her tightly. Something like a growl rumbled in my throat until I caught myself.

Then Felicia and Luna, hand in hand, joined the dance, lifting their knees, stamping the ground, circling the fire. I knew Felicia loved to dance, was always trying to get me to go along, but this couldn't have been what she'd had in mind.

There seemed no end to the dancing. Women whirled like dervishes, skipping and prancing around the fire. If Felicia was pretending, if she was just going along, then she was one hell of an actress. She danced with as much abandon as the others around the slowly dying fire, whipping her hair around, throwing her arms up to the skies. Luna stopped at some point, and I spotted her by the porch of the ranch house, her hands on her hips, her breath coming hard still, watching the proceedings with a satisfied smile on her face. God, I wanted to slap her. I wanted to race down there, scoop Felicia up in my arms, carry her away from this madness.

Reasons touched my arm.

"Let's get out of here," he said. "We've seen enough."

"I haven't."

"Yes, you have. They clearly don't mean to harm Felicia. Every minute we sit up here, we're putting her in danger."

I hesitated. He was right, of course, but it felt like abandonment. How could I leave her when she was in this much jeopardy?

I peered through the binoculars again, spotted Felicia in the frenzied crowd. Her head was thrown back; she was laughing, jumping around. Okay, so she didn't look like she was in danger, didn't seem to be afraid. Did that mean she was brainwashed? Was she lost to me forever?

Reasons tugged on my sleeve. "Come on."

I sighed, put the binoculars in their case. Reasons gathered up his stuff, and we slunk away through the trees.

SEVENTEEN
■ ◆ ■

Maybe Reasons was accustomed to fasting, but I wasn't. We hadn't eaten all day. I stopped at the first restaurant I spotted on the way back into Taos, in the little roadside burg of El Prado. It was called Mamacita's Café, and it was definitely a place for locals. Pickup trucks filled the narrow gravel parking lot that circled the wooden building, which was shedding its dried white paint like dandruff. Neon beer signs cluttered the small windows. Inside, vinyl booths lined the walls and rickety tables filled the center of the room.

The place was populated almost entirely by men in greasy baseball caps and faded jeans, many of them still caked with the sweat and grime from whatever they'd done all day for a living. We fit right in.

I led Reasons to a booth in the corner, as far away from prying eyes and ears as possible in the small café. A middle-aged waitress with henna hair and a slash of red lipstick dropped off two menus without saying anything, then hurried off with a coffeepot to fill cups around the room.

One look at the menu told me Reasons would have trouble finding anything to meet his vegetarian requirements. Tough.

I was starving. By the time the lipsticked waitress returned to our table, I was ready to order everything on the menu.

Lipstick pulled her ticket pad from her pocket, looked us over.

"You're new," she said.

"Just visiting," I said.

"Don't get many tourists in here."

"We're not tourists. We're looking for work."

If she was at all interested in us as potential date material, the thought of another unemployed man turned her off. She shifted a wad of gum in her cheek.

"You ready to order?"

"You bet."

I ordered what looked like the biggest combination plate on the menu, along with chips and salsa, beer. Reasons asked for blue corn enchiladas. I guess cheese didn't have a soul for him to fret over.

As the waitress gathered the menus, she looked at me again. "What happened to your eye?"

No one had asked about the shiner for so long, I'd more or less forgotten it was there. I'd noticed in the mirror that morning that it had gone from purple to a sort of yellow-green, the color of the yolk in a hard-boiled egg.

"Dining accident," I said. "I'm still learning to eat with a knife and fork."

Lipstick cracked her gum, didn't smile.

"Well, try not to get blood all over the table."

She drifted away to take our orders to the kitchen. Once she was out of earshot, Reasons said, "You're amazing."

"I know, but why do you say that?"

"We come from an induction ceremony for the woman you love, and you're flirting with this tart of a waitress."

I shifted in my seat.

"It's automatic. Flirting with the waitress is an American tradition."

He shook his head, as if that was one tradition he could live without.

"So what about that ceremony?" I said. "You learn anything from it?"

"Typical pagan rite—fire, dancing, sage stick. If Felicia is tricking them, she's certainly doing a good job."

"You think they got to her?"

"Hard to say. I'd have to talk to her to tell. Look in her eyes. See if there's fervor there."

Just like I see it in your eyes, I thought. That glossy faraway look that means you've gone beyond whatever is in front of you. That electrified expression that says you've plugged into the God Circuit.

The waitress brought our drinks. I smiled my thanks, but she didn't smile back. She'd probably used up her life's allotment of smiles years ago, wasting them on goons like me.

Once she was out of earshot, I said to Reasons, "You're the expert. What do you think we should do now?"

He studied me for a minute, a smile playing at his lips.

"I never thought I'd hear you call me an expert at anything."

"Hey, I'm out of my league here. You know these cults. Is there anything we can do?"

"I'd suggest that we pray, but I know that's not what you mean."

"Damned right."

"You're a man of action, Bubba, whether you realize it or not. You want to *do* something, no matter what, in every situation. Sometimes, there truly is nothing you can do but wait. If Felicia has succeeded in tricking them, if she still has her head together, then she'll find her way out when she's ready."

"And if that's not the case?"

"Then maybe we can go in and get her at some point, just like we'd planned to do with Margaret. But I don't think that's wise now."

"So we just wait."

He nodded. "We can keep watching them, if you want. I'm willing to stick it out. But it'll mean trouble if we're caught."

"I know, I know. But we have to do something, and surveillance is the only thing that comes to mind."

The waitress arrived with the steaming platters of food.

"That was quick." I meant it as a compliment.

"Yeah, our cook's fast," she said. "He's just not very good."

I tore into my platter, munching and crunching. The cook might not have been a gourmet, but it tasted good to me. Reasons even showed a little more relish than usual as he nibbled away.

I said nothing more until my plate was nearly cleaned, and I took a second to come up for air.

"Ah, that's better. My stomach was so empty, it thought my throat had been cut."

Reasons grinned, wiped a string of cheese off his chin.

"Next time we go up to WOMB, we should take some food," he said. "It makes for a long day if you're hungry."

"I was afraid my growling stomach was going to give us away."

He chuckled. Rarely had I seen him so happy. It was as if he'd sensed that he'd won my trust, that he'd dropped down the list of suspects a few rungs just because he'd stuck it out with me all day.

Whom else did I have to trust? Aside from Reasons, I was alone up here. One man against forty women. And they had the law on their side.

A couple of good old boys fell into the booth next to us, so we said nothing more about WOMB. We mopped up our plates, left money on the table to cover the tab, and headed for the door.

As we stepped out into the cool night air, Reasons said, "You know, Bubba, we shouldn't worry so much about what to do next. God will show us the way."

I turned to scold him, but I got distracted by a truck engine revving in the parking lot. Something familiar about that mufflerless roar. I wheeled just as the truck rocketed forward, heading toward us. It was a gray Ford with ladder racks.

"Down!"

"What?"

I grabbed at Reasons's arm as I lunged backward toward the café door, but I missed. He stood there blinking at the headlights, no idea what was coming.

"Get down!"

I scrambled backward on my hands and feet and butt, my eyes on the truck as it rumbled past. The business end of a crossbow snaked out the passenger window, there was a whoosh in the air; then the truck fishtailed away, throwing gravel. It lurched onto the highway and roared off.

I leaped to my feet, tried to see a license plate, but there was none. The truck was gone.

Reasons lay at my feet. I crouched beside him to see if he was hurt.

"Purvis?"

He opened his mouth, but no words came out. Red bubbles streamed from his lips.

"Oh shit!"

He'd caught the short arrow in the throat. Maybe two inches of it protruded from under his chin. I tried to get my hand under his head to cradle it, found blood pooling on the gravel.

"Help! Help, somebody!"

The waitress stuck her head out the door.

"What the hell's going on out there?"

"Call an ambulance. Quick! My friend's been hurt!"

She disappeared back inside. Customers trickled out the door into the parking lot, but I paid them no mind.

"Purvis, can you hear me? Hang in there."

I could see in his eyes that he was slipping away, that he could no longer see me, though I was right there in his face. He felt around with one hand, found my arm, grabbed it and squeezed. He managed to smile at the contact. Then his eyes rolled back in his head, and he was gone.

E I G H T E E N
■ ◆ ■

I still sat there, washed in the blood of Reasons, when an ambulance shrieked into the parking lot, lights flashing. Two paramedics in pale blue uniforms bounded out of the ambulance, shouting, "Stand back! Give us room!" Customers from the café had clustered tightly around me, gawking and shaking their heads, but I hadn't even noticed.

One of the paramedics, a middle-aged Hispanic man, touched my shoulder. "Where are you hurt?"

I shrugged his hand away.

"I'm not hurt. And you're too late. He's dead."

He grabbed my shoulder, rougher now, pulled me backward. "Let us check him out."

They crouched over Reasons's body, one of them pressing a stethoscope to his chest. Their eyes met and both shook their heads, confirming what I already knew.

"What the hell happened here?" demanded the other paramedic, a pimply-faced guy whose long hair probably defied all regulations. "What is that in his throat?"

"Crossbow," I croaked. "Somebody shot him."

The paramedic rocked back on his heels, looked to the crowd. "Somebody call the sheriff."

Lipstick, the waitress, stepped forward. "Already done it. They're on their way."

The paramedics stepped back from the body, moving gingerly, as if they might disturb evidence. This, after they'd parked their ambulance right in the middle of whatever tire tracks the pickup truck might've left.

Reasons's blood was sticky on my hands. The right side of my shirt was soaked with it, as were the knees of my jeans. The dark blood made me shudder. I had to get it off me. I turned to push my way through the crowd, but the onlookers parted, giving me a wide berth.

"Where are you going?" the young paramedic shouted. "You stay right here!"

I ignored him, went into the café. A man in a cook's apron stood behind the counter, not leaving the cash register to go gape with the others. He gasped at the sight of me.

I found the rest room. It was filthy, so I didn't mind getting pink water everywhere as I washed the blood from my hands. I stripped off my shirt, held it under the running water, then washed my stomach where the blood clung to me. Nothing could be done about my jeans, unless I was willing to walk around in my underwear, so I left the stains there.

I took some comfort in cleaning up, as if washing would help erase what had just happened. I soaped my hands and rinsed them, soaped them again, rinsed. The blood caked in my cuticles. I picked at it under the running water, getting lost in the effort. Anything to keep from thinking about Reasons lying out there, the life knocked out of him.

Someone hammered on the door.

"Go away. I'm busy."

The door burst open, and a deputy crouched in the doorway, his gun drawn, looking for someone to shoot. I held up my dripping hands.

"What the hell are you doing?"

"I had blood on me. I had to wash it off."

"That blood might've been evidence!"

"There's plenty more of it out there, asshole."

"Watch your mouth, boy!"

The deputy was a ruddy older fellow, with no lips and a jaw like an anvil. I imagined he'd rearranged a few smart mouths over his career.

I picked up my wet shirt, which caused the deputy to draw a bead on me again.

"It's just a shirt."

"Come out of there!"

The young paramedic appeared at the cop's elbow, muttering, "He may be in shock. That might be why he's acting strangely."

"I don't give a rat's ass. He's under arrest until I say different."

The deputy marched me out through the café, through the crowd that had grown bigger outside. The paramedics had draped a white sheet over Reasons's body, and it was busy soaking up his blood.

His gun still trained on me, the deputy circled ahead, popped open the back door of his squad car. As I moved to duck inside, another patrol car roared into the parking lot, lights flashing. Sheriff Hernandez got out from behind the wheel.

"Hold on, John," he shouted. "Bring him over here."

I obediently marched over, met Hernandez in front of his car, the headlights slashing through our legs, throwing white beams toward Reasons's corpse and the crowd beyond.

"Bubba Mabry," the sheriff said. "I should've known."

"Someone killed Reasons," I said. "Shot him with a crossbow."

"A crossbow? You sure?"

"I saw it happen. I yelled for him to get down, but he just froze there. It hit him in the throat."

"Where was the killer?"

"In a truck. It was a drive-by. He's long gone."

"Helluva shot with a crossbow. You said 'he.' It was a man who did it?"

The thought hadn't clearly registered until now. I'd gotten a glimpse of the killer, just a silhouette really, as I was crab-walking out of harm's way.

"I didn't really get a look at the driver," I said. "But I'm pretty sure he had a beard."

Sheriff Hernandez drummed his fingers on the hood of his car.

"A beard, huh? Guess that would rule out your friends up at WOMB."

My teeth ground together. I hadn't really had a chance to think about who might've killed Purvis Reasons. A crossbow sure seemed like the type of weapon a WOMBster would use, would fit with the bows and spears we'd seen at their ranch. But I'd seen what I'd seen, and there'd been a beard.

"I guess a woman could wear a false beard," I said. "I really didn't get that good a look. It happened so fast."

"All right." Hernandez reached out, clasped me by the elbow to turn me. "We'll talk it through some more at the office. Just get in my car for now."

I sat in the backseat while Hernandez shouted instructions to his deputies and the paramedics. I didn't pay attention to what he said. I was too lost in thought.

Who would want Reasons dead? Or was the arrow intended for me? If the driver of the rattling truck was a man, could he have a connection to WOMB? That didn't seem possible. If Luna wanted someone killed, there were plenty of beefy, well-armed women she could call upon. Why a man? And if the killer had no connection to WOMB, who was he? Reasons and I hadn't worked on anything else, hadn't crossed anyone else since we came to Taos. Could it have been someone from Reasons's past? Some disgruntled cultist who wanted him removed? But the same truck had made a try on my life earlier, nearly running me down. It must've been me he was after. Reasons was dead because my reflexes were better than his.

I hadn't really allowed myself to think much about the truck trying to run me down, figuring it was a scare tactic more than a true murder attempt. Probably the same sick fuck who'd put that rubber snake in my bed. I'd attributed both events to WOMB, their little way of running me out of town. But this was different; this was deadly. And there'd been a man behind the wheel.

Hernandez climbed into the squad car, cranked up the engine, wheeled us back around toward town. The car's air conditioner blew fiercely, and I crossed my arms over my bare, damp chest.

"You cold?" Hernandez spoke to me via the mirror.

"A little. Why?"

"You're teeth are chattering."

"I'm kind of shaky. That paramedic said I might be in shock."

"You might be. You want me to swing by the hospital so they can check you out?"

"Naw, I'll be all right."

I wrapped my arms tighter around my body, holding myself together.

"You feel like talking?" he asked. "You want to tell me what happened out there?"

I didn't feel like it in the least, but I found my mouth spewing words on its own.

"As Reasons and I walked out of the café, a truck zoomed toward us. I recognized the truck and shouted for him to get down as I scrambled out of the way. I saw a crossbow come out the passenger-side window and then, pow, Reasons went down. I jumped up to try to get a look at the license plate, but there wasn't one. Then I realized Reasons had been hit. He died in just a minute or two. I guess the arrow hit an artery. There was a lot of blood."

As I talked, my voice got croakier. I tried to swallow, but it was impossible. I hung my head, waited for the grief to pass.

Hernandez waited until I looked up again before he spoke.

"How did you recognize the truck?"

"What?"

"The truck. You said you recognized it. Who does it belong to?"

"I don't know."

"But you recognized it."

"Yeah. Same truck made a run at me a couple of nights ago."

"It did? Why didn't you report it?"

"Didn't I tell you about it when we talked?"

"No."

"You sure?"

"I'm sure."

Something clicked in my head. I'd told Felicia about nearly getting run down by the truck, but I'd kept that little tidbit from the sheriff. I had to clear my head, get my story straight. This was no time to be confused.

We pulled into the gravel parking lot of the sheriff's office. Hernandez got out, opened my door, walked me into his office. I still carried my dripping shirt. He noticed it, took it away from me, handed it to a deputy at the booking desk.

"Bag that and stow it somewhere," he told the deputy. "Get a shirt from the jail-uniform stock and bring it to my office."

We went into Hernandez's now-familiar office and I perched on one of his wooden chairs, feeling naked and vulnerable. Hernandez, to his credit, asked no more questions until the deputy appeared with the shirt and I had a chance to cover up. The shirt was bright orange, too big, and had *Taos County Jail* stenciled across the back, but I took comfort in it nonetheless.

Once I was settled, Hernandez picked up a pencil, leaned across his desk, and said, "Now tell me about this truck."

I talked. Boy, did I talk. I talked to Hernandez, to his chief investigator, to a flinty state policeman who joined us later. I told them everything, still too stunned and confused to play wise with them. I told them about the truck with the rattling ladder racks, about the surreptitious trips to WOMB Reasons and I had made, about Felicia Quattlebaum going undercover among the pagans. I begged them not to blow her cover, but they said there was nothing they could do anyway if a reporter had joined WOMB of her own volition. I had nothing to show that she'd been brainwashed or that she was in danger.

I told them again about the rubber snake, about Jeronimo Valdez's cattle mutilations, about how I'd considered Reasons a suspect in Margaret Ogletroop's slaying. I told them everything I knew about the Ogletroops, about Purvis Reasons, about Felicia. I even told the truth about how I got the black eye.

Hernandez, for his part, was solicitous and kind. No yelling, no demanding. He had a deputy fetch coffee for me, gave the hard eye to other investigators whenever they seemed too stern with me. I talked and I talked. Dawn leaked light through the windows by the time I ran out of things to say.

The sheriff leaned back in his chair, stretched the kinks out of his shoulders, and yawned.

"Can you think of anything else?"

I shook my head wearily.

"Not unless you want to know my shoe size or where I went to elementary school."

He managed a tired smile, tilting his head toward the door to tell the others in the room to leave.

After they closed the door, he said, "You know, Bubba, I

143

should probably lock you up as a public nuisance. You've been in town—what, five days? And there have been two murders. That's more than we'd normally get in three or four months around here. You're trouble, no question about it."

What could I say? I nodded, sighed.

"Could I at least have a cell all to myself? I feel like I need to sleep for about three days straight."

Hernandez's brilliant smile split his face again.

"I'm not going to lock you up. I don't see any reason to, though those other officers might think different."

He was right. The others had seemed ready to put me away, just because I'd kept them up all night.

"I think you've told us everything you know," he continued. "If you knew who fired that arrow, you'd have already told us, right?"

"You know it."

"All right, then, here's what I want you to do. I'll have a deputy drive you over to the café to pick up your car, and I want you to go straight to the Holiday Inn, climb into your bed, and don't get out of it. Are you okay to drive?"

"I'll be all right."

He led me out to the booking area and found a deputy he called Red to give me a lift.

"And Bubba," he said as I was going out the door, "try not to get anyone else killed, okay? We need a break."

N I N E T E E N
■ ◆ ■

The squad car followed me all the way back to the motel, probably making sure I didn't fall asleep at the wheel and run down some tourists. I pretended I didn't see it as I let myself into my room.

I stripped off the jail shirt and my jeans, which had gone stiff in the knees from the bloodstains. I sat in a chair in my underwear, my head humming with all the words I'd spewed in the past few hours.

After a while, I peeked out between the curtains to see if Red still watched. I saw him get out of his squad car and speak through the window of an unmarked car that clearly had come to take his place. Then Red drove away, leaving the plain brown wrapper to watch me.

Never had a bed looked so inviting. It called to me, pleaded with me to come enjoy its caresses, but I shook my head at it, irritated by the temptation. I took a long, hot shower, found some nearly clean jeans and a shirt to wear, then got together my gun and my binoculars. As my mother always says, There's plenty of time to sleep when you're in your grave. I had to get back out to WOMB.

The lawman in the unmarked Dodge tried to look unsurprised when I stepped out through the door into the bright sunshine. He glanced away as if to say, Oh, no, I haven't been watching your room, but he kept cutting his eyes my way as I climbed behind the wheel of the Chevy. He followed me out of the parking lot, keeping close so he wouldn't lose me.

I drove straight to the sheriff's office, which was probably the last thing the tail expected. I parked in the shade of the big cottonwood near the street, then strolled around the building, toward the door of the sheriff's office, as if I'd remembered something I needed to report.

The unmarked Dodge swung around to the far side of the building, parking with the rest of the cop cars. I ducked into a crouch and slipped between cars, making my way back to the Chevy.

When I reached my car, I popped to a standing position just long enough to scan the parking lot. No sign of the plainclothes cop. Probably still inside the building, hunting me. Had to hurry. I climbed behind the wheel, fumbled the key into the ignition, and cranked the engine. It groaned, muttered. Oh no. Not now. I cranked it again. It coughed and sputtered, couldn't get its breath. Shit. I hammered the dash with my fist. The plainclothesman must know by now that I didn't really go into the building. He's probably running for his car. I pressed the gas pedal all the way to the floor and turned the key so hard, it nearly twisted off in the lock. The Chevy got the message, caught, sputtered, caught again, then rumbled to an idle. I slammed it into gear and actually burned rubber when I hit the street.

I drove out toward WOMB, so busy watching my mirrors that I weaved all over the road. No sign of the unmarked Dodge. I'd given him the slip.

I turned onto the road that climbed up to the Valdez ranch, bounced along with the trees and wildflowers blurring past on either side. Old man Valdez sat in his rocking chair on the porch. I waved and so did he. He stood up, as if expecting me to join him, but I kept going. I let myself through his gate, then jumped back into the car without looking toward the house. I didn't want to get tangled up in a long-winded conversation with him. I wanted to get to WOMB, to check on Felicia, maybe find a way to get word to her of Reasons's death. There was a killer on the loose, one that might be connected to WOMB, and she needed to know.

Besides, maybe if she knew Reasons had been killed, she'd stop this crazy undercover plan and run off to write a story about him. Whatever. I wanted her out of there.

I left the Chevy in the usual spot, clambered down the hill alongside the granite outcrop. I tried to be quiet, but my haste and my lack of sleep had me stumbling along, tripping over rocks and walking into low branches. I passed the altar where Margaret Ogletroop had been slain, passed the bowl of boulders where Reasons and I had watched Felicia's induction ceremony.

Emboldened by sleeplessness, I walked right up to WOMB, within sight of the ranch house, and crouched behind some bushes that grew around the base of a cottonwood tree at the edge of the clearing. The stream burbled a lullaby to my right. Behind me were more trees I could escape into if I was spotted. I stretched out on my stomach, propped up on my elbows, and watched the compound wake up.

Women tumbled out of the tepees, stretching and yawning. Some went to the ranch house—for breakfast, I guessed. One came to fetch a pail of water from the stream, so close to me, I could see her dangling earrings and her unshaven armpits. I held my breath and lay perfectly still. She turned and went about her business without ever looking my way.

Smoke trailed out the ranch house's chimney as women walked back and forth across the compound, going to the outhouse, the henhouse, a greenhouse. Wonderful aromas of cooking food—eggs and onions and bread—wafted my way on a light breeze. My stomach rumbled. I hadn't thought to bring food with me, or water, or anything. I had a set of binoculars I didn't need and a gun I probably wouldn't use and a headache that wouldn't go away. That was it.

I whiled away the morning watching the compound and thinking about Reasons and cursing myself. No matter how I looked at it, I found it easy to blame myself for his death. I should've jumped sideways and taken him down with me as the crossbow aimed our way. I should've been more careful about being followed. It was no coincidence that the rattling truck found us at Mamacita's Café. The killer must've been following us off and on since that first night I spotted him, when he nearly creamed me in the middle of the street. I'd never seen the truck behind us, had rarely even thought about the possibility of being tailed. I should've paid better attention, but I'd been so caught up in worrying about Felicia, I hadn't worried about Reasons and me.

As irritating as Reasons had been, I missed him. All the times I'd thought about getting rid of him, nothing like this had ever crossed my mind. He didn't deserve to die. Nobody does.

My thoughts were interrupted by the sight of Felicia stepping out onto the ranch house porch, hand in hand with Luna. My heart sank at the sight of them, standing so close, with no awkwardness between them. Like lovers.

I couldn't hear what she was saying, but Luna appeared to be showing Felicia the perimeter of WOMB, pointing up into the trees on the hillside, down the dirt track toward the road. Felicia took it all in, looking interested and bright-eyed, the way she hardly ever looks for me.

What if she's fallen for Luna? How would I compete? The love between two women always had seemed so mysterious and exclusive. They know things only women know, can touch in ways only women know to touch. The thought of them together was almost more than I could stand. I nearly called out, but my throat was constricted too tightly for words to pass. I pulled one knee up under me, ready to do what, I'm not sure. Whatever it was, the urge disappeared as soon as Judah stepped out onto the porch with them. A mad dash toward that mountain of a woman could only end in pain and humiliation.

Luna whispered something to Felicia, breathing right into her ear, and they turned and went back to the house. That whispered message gave me something to fret over for the next couple of hours while I watched the compound go about its everyday life. I saw nothing more of Felicia or Luna.

It was hot and itchy under the bushes. I yearned to roll down the creek bank, splash into the water like an alligator. I was thirsty and hungry and stiff from lying still so long. And nothing happened. If there'd been something interesting to watch, even another one of those fearful rituals, the time wouldn't have crawled past so slowly. But there was nothing, just the occasional woman gathering firewood, running errands, or going to the outhouse. The boredom started getting to me, and I got careless. I fell asleep.

Fell is the right word for it. One minute, I was lying there, wide awake and reasonably alert, despite being up all night at the sheriff's office. The next thing I knew, someone was yanking my gun from my holster. I bolted upright, wheeled around, to find five women standing around me. They must've been headed to the swimming hole, because some of them still held their towels. Judah was with them. She held a spear, and my gun.

"You again." She snorted, barely containing herself. "Damn, you're easy to capture."

I shrugged, yawned.

149

"I must've gone to sleep."

"Some private eye you are."

"I had a rough night."

She gave me the hard eye.

"Where's your friend?"

"My friend? Oh, you mean Reasons?"

"Yeah, where is he?"

"He's dead."

"Sure he is."

"No, he is. Someone killed him last night."

"I don't believe you."

I shrugged again. "Believe whatever you want. Go hunt for him in the woods, for all I care. You won't find him unless you look in the morgue."

"On your feet."

I obliged, my knees popping and every joint creaking. The other women stepped away, keeping their eyes on me in case I tried something. I thought about what that might be. I certainly wasn't going to try to wrest the spear away from Judah. That would be the surest way to end up a Bubba kabob.

The stream tumbled behind me, cutting off any but the slowest, splashiest escapes. The main clearing of WOMB was off to my right. No chance there. In fact, I didn't see any escape, and I didn't really care. My head was foggy from sleep; my reactions were slow as a lizard's on a cold day. If Judah wanted to take me into WOMB for more lectures and humiliations, fine. I was tired of watching the place, anyway. If Luna wanted to parade me in front of her troops while we waited for the sheriff, fine again. Maybe I could at least get word to Felicia about Reasons and the killer. I might even be able to do it without tipping them to Felicia's real identity. Then again, with me there's always the possibility of a serious flub, which just might get us both killed.

Judah marched me into the compound at spear-point. The

would-be swimmers followed, clutching their towels, wide-eyed at the persistent man in their midst. As before, the WOMBsters spilled out into the clearing to watch, muttering and shooting me threatening looks. We walked up to the porch of the ranch house as Luna and Felicia emerged from inside. Luna held her hand, but Felicia gently pulled away when she saw me, an automatic reaction that I hoped didn't send some message to Luna. I tried not to stare at Felicia, but it was hard. I wanted to read her eyes, to see whether she was still mine.

"So," Luna trumpeted, "you've come back to see us."

"I found him asleep in some bushes over there," Judah said behind me.

"Asleep?"

"I got bored."

"Is that so? We're not interesting enough for you, eh? Maybe we can spice things up."

"Don't go to any trouble."

She grinned mischievously. "Oh, it won't be any trouble for us. And, I guarantee you, it'll keep your attention."

She turned to one of her lieutenants, the one she'd called Selena, and whispered in her ear. Felicia played the same game with her eyes that I had, trying not to make contact with me, trying not to give anything away. Knowing Felicia, it was probably all she could do to keep her mouth shut. She loves to lecture me when I mess up.

Selena grabbed the arms of two other women standing nearby, and the three of them disappeared around the side of the house.

Luna crossed her arms under her breasts, cocked a hip, all sauce and spunk as she studied me. I found myself letting my eyes run down her round body, then forced myself to stop. The woman exuded sexuality, earthiness. No wonder she was the leader. No wonder half the women of WOMB were attracted to her. Was Felicia? I glanced over at her again, but she was making a concerted effort to appear uninterested in my presence.

"Where's your loudmouthed sidekick?" Luna asked.

"Purvis Reasons is no longer among the living."

"What do you mean?"

"He told me the same thing," Judah said from behind me. "He said the other man was killed last night."

Out of the corner of my eye, I saw Felicia's head whip around at this news.

"In fact," I added smugly, "the sheriff will probably be rolling up here any minute to question you about the murder."

"We had nothing to do with it," said Luna.

"Tell it to the law."

"We're not killers," she said, "despite the way you've tried to portray us to the sheriff."

"I never said you killed anybody. Though you have to admit, marching people around at the point of a spear is pretty suspicious."

I cocked my head to look over my shoulder at Judah, who gave me a vicious jab in the kidney with the butt of the spear. That got my head turned back around.

"I don't really think you killed Reasons, either," I said. "I think it was a man who did it."

Luna flashed her wicked smile again.

"That would make sense, wouldn't it? Men are always the ones who kill, the ones who war, the ones who rape. They're victims in a way—victims of their own aggressive hormones, which keep them from being gentle or kind or loving."

A murmur of agreement rippled through the WOMBsters.

"Purvis Reasons was gentle," I said flatly. "Now, he's dead."

"Which proves my point precisely."

She nodded to herself, declaring herself the winner of this verbal joust. I let her have her victory. No use getting them more stirred up. I couldn't think of any response, anyway.

Selena and the other two came around the corner of the house, carrying a rough-hewn wooden table. They set it in the center of the clearing, near the ash heap from the ritual fire. One of them carefully spread a tarp over it, as if she was ready to set a picnic.

"All right, Judah," Luna said. "You know what to do."

Judah grabbed my arm, spun me around, dragged me roughly over to the table.

"Climb up there," she said.

"Up there?"

Rather than debate it, she grabbed me under the arms and tossed me up onto the table like a sack of manure.

"Lie down on your back."

Why argue? What could they possibly do? Luna had just preached about how they weren't killers. And if they weren't going to kill me, how bad could it be?

One of the women handed Judah a coil of hemp rope and she tied me spread-eagled on the table, wrists and ankles firmly secured to the table legs by pieces she cut off the coil with a bowie knife she'd pulled from her belt.

Okay, I'm thinking, they're going to leave me to bake in the sun a while. I can handle that. Might even get some sleep.

Luna and the others crowded near the table, a mass of female anger, buzzing around me like bees.

"Give me the knife, Judah." Judah handed over the foot-long blade. Luna raised it above her head in both hands, like an offering to the sky.

"Bless this knife, O Goddess," she said. "Bless its holy work."

"Whoa, now," I said. "I thought you weren't killers."

"We're not going to kill you," she said, lowering the knife. "We're going to rid you of your awful testosterone, the evil hormones that make you a man."

I don't know much about anatomy, so it took me a second to puzzle it through. But when the realization dawned, my scrotum shriveled, tried to crawl up inside my belly.

"And, to complete Sister Felicia's induction, we're going to let her do the honors."

Felicia had hung back at the edge of the crowd, but the other women grabbed her and pushed her forward until she stood beside Luna, looking down at me, expressionless.

"This is wrong, Luna," I said. "Don't do this. I'm not some bull you can make into a steer. I'm a human being."

Luna sneered into my face. "You're a *man.*"

She handed the big knife to Felicia, who took it with trembling hands. Luna leaned over me, her dark hair draping down over her face, and began unfastening the button on my jeans.

Her head snapped back as Felicia grabbed a handful of her hair. Felicia reached under her chin, laid the shiny blade against her Adam's apple.

"Let him go," she said, her voice low and under control. "Cut him loose or I'll slit your throat."

The women around us gasped, stepped back. Judah growled, tried to move around the table to get her hands on Felicia. Felicia yanked Luna's head around toward Judah.

"Do what she says, Judah," Luna rasped. "Untie him."

Judah fumbled at the knots in the ropes, too busy cutting her eyes toward Felicia and Luna to pay attention to what she was doing. As soon as I was free, I scrambled down off the table and snatched my revolver from the back of Judah's belt.

"Okay, back up, all of you," I said, my voice shaky. "Give us some room."

They obeyed, though several snarled and spat threats my way.

"Come here, Felicia," I said.

Felicia backed around the table, still holding tight to Luna, until she was beside me. Then she took the knife from the witch's neck and pushed her away. Luna sprawled across the table with an *oof*.

"This way, Bubba." Felicia took off, running toward the road.

I followed, jogging backward to keep my eye on the crowd, then turning to run full tilt toward the trees, glancing over my shoulder to make sure they weren't pursuing.

We ran across the rickety bridge over the creek, plunged into the trees on the other side. I looked back once more, but they weren't following. They still stood around the table, Luna watching us go, her hands on her hips. Then she threw back her head and laughed heartily. The others joined in, and gales of laughter chased us all the way to Felicia's car.

TWENTY

■ ◆ ■

"God, you were great back there!"

Felicia couldn't keep from grinning. "I have to admit, it was a rush. I'd had enough of that woman, anyway. Holding a knife to her neck felt pretty good."

"You were just great. I was starting to get scared, and then, boom, you were all over her."

"Scared? You?"

"I know that's hard to believe."

"What did you think, that I'd really cut your jewels off?"

"No, not really, but I wasn't certain what was going to happen. Reasons had me believing that maybe they'd brainwashed you."

"Some brains are too dirty to wash."

She laughed, weaving all over the road as we raced back toward town. High on adrenaline, glad to be free of WOMB.

I was pretty high myself. Not only had I escaped with my testosterone intact but I had Felicia back.

"I'm just glad to have you out of there," I said. "I was worried about you."

"I can take care of myself."

"Took pretty good care of me, too. This time, at least."

Felicia snorted.

"Somebody has to look after you. Falling asleep in the bushes while on stakeout!"

Here we go.

"I know. Quite a gaffe. But I have a good excuse. I was up all night at the sheriff's office."

I told her about Reasons catching the arrow, about the all-night interrogation with Hernandez and friends, about slipping the tail so I could return to WOMB and check on her.

"You guys watched me out there the whole time?"

"Not the whole time. But a lot of it. We saw you get inducted."

Felicia actually blushed. "All that dancing?"

"Mm-hmm. You seemed to be enjoying yourself."

"I was just playing along with them. It was all an act."

"You're one heck of an actress."

"All right, I'll admit that I kind of got into the dancing, all that whirling by the fire, with the forest all around. It was fun."

"Watching you, I started to think it was so much fun, you might stay there."

"Are you kidding? All that New Age mumbo jumbo all the time? It was all I could do not to laugh in their faces."

Now that's the woman I know and love.

"And another thing. Nobody smokes at WOMB. I haven't had a cigarette since I sneaked one late last night. Find my purse in the backseat and dig out those Marlboros, will you?"

I obliged, then watched her light up and inhale deeply.

"Ah, that's better." She filled the little Toyota with smoke, and we rolled down our windows. "Luna's lucky I didn't go ahead and cut her just because she stood between me and my cigarettes."

Felicia still drove at top speed. Fancy adobe homes and grazing horses and little inns blurred past.

"Was it worth it?" I asked her. "Did you learn anything that made it worth the risk of going undercover?"

Felicia shrugged, took another drag from the cigarette.

"I learned a lot about WOMB, what they believe and why they're living way the hell up here. But I didn't learn squat about Margaret Ogletroop's murder, except I don't think they did it."

"No?"

"Nah, they're all too much into sisterhood and collective consciousness and Mother Earth. They don't even eat meat. If one of their chickens dies of natural causes, they give it a decent burial."

"Killing a chicken is one thing. One of them killing Margaret out of jealousy or anger might be something else."

"Maybe. But if there's a renegade among them, she didn't reveal herself to me."

Felicia lit a new cigarette with the ember of the first, then blithely threw the smoldering butt out her window. I glanced back, expecting to see a prairie fire erupting.

"So did you get enough to write a story about WOMB?"

"Oh yeah. That's where we're going now, in case you're wondering. I've still got time to make the first edition."

"You, uh, you're not going to mention me in this story, are you?"

She squinted at me through her cloud of smoke.

"Maybe. Why?"

"Well, it's just sort of embarrassing. Getting caught like that. Coming very close to having my privates court-martialed."

She grinned.

"I don't think the *Gazette* would print that part," she said. "And I don't think it was real, anyway."

"Real? It seemed real enough to me. You weren't the one trussed up on the picnic table."

"No, Bubba, think about it. It was too easy. They let us walk out of there."

"That knife you were waving around seemed to have a lot to do with that."

"Exactly. Why give the knife to the new recruit? If Luna was serious about hurting you, she'd have done it herself."

"So why did they put us through all that?"

"A joke, Bubba. You heard them laughing. They were—pardon the expression—pulling your leg."

That gave me something to chew on while we drove the rest of the way to the Holiday Inn.

Felicia set up shop in my room, eating cigarettes and pounding away at her little keyboard at a table by the windows. I tried to look over her shoulder, but that irritated her, so I moped around the room, sipping a Coke, watching her work.

When she was done writing, she transmitted the story back to the newspaper over the telephone. Then she got on the phone herself, barking instructions to her editor, arguing against any change in the story.

When she finally hung up, I ventured, "You didn't put me in your story?"

"No, I didn't."

I whewed in relief. I'd been embarrassed in print enough for one lifetime. If my buddies on the Cruise heard about my near sacrifice at WOMB, I'd never live it down.

"I appreciate it."

"I didn't do it for you. It was too hinky, our word against theirs. The *Gazette* would require something from the official record, and I figured you wouldn't want to file a report with the sheriff."

"You got that right. I got the feeling Sheriff Hernandez will lock me up on sight next time, just for being a pain in the ass."

"Now, Bubba, you know being a pain in the ass is no felony. Otherwise, you'd have been doing time long ago."

Well, I couldn't just let her get away with that. I chased her around the room, growling and tickling, while she shrieked with laughter. One thing led to another, and before long we were lying in the bed, catching our breath, Felicia still giggling, me panting and sweating from the lovemaking.

Felicia had been more aggressive than usual, and I couldn't help but wonder whether it was pent-up arousal from two days of holding hands with Luna.

"Felicia?" I said after a while. "Did that woman try to seduce you?"

She gave me a coy look, eyebrow cocked. "You mean Luna?"

"Of course I mean Luna."

"Would it make you insecure if she had?"

"It sure as hell would."

She giggled again, couldn't contain herself.

"So that's the real reason you spent all that time watching me from the woods."

"Now I didn't say that. I was concerned about your safety—"

"You were worried you'd lose me to some witchy woman."

"No, I wasn't. It wasn't that at all."

She crossed her arms over the sheet, trying not to grin as she watched me flounder.

"Okay, I was worried about it. What if she persuaded you? What if you found her attractive? How would I win you back?"

She snuggled up against me, draped an arm over my chest.

"You don't have to win me, Bubba. I'm not some kind of prize. I *choose* to be with you. And I always will."

"Really?"

"Well, unless somebody better comes along."

I hit her with my pillow.

TWENTY-ONE

■◆■

Wednesday morning, the phone jangled us awake. I pulled a pillow over my head, but Felicia picked up the receiver.

"It's for you."

I took the receiver, dragged it under the pillow to my ear.

"Yeah?"

"Bubba, it's Marcus Ogletroop."

I sat straight up, nearly dropped the phone, then fumbled it back to my ear.

"Good morning, Mr. Ogletroop."

Felicia goggled her eyes at me, then slipped out of bed, naked, and padded off to the bathroom. I watched her go while I inquired why Ogletroop was calling at the crack of dawn.

"I got a full report from the sheriff on Mr. Reasons's death," Ogletroop said. "We're making arrangements to have his body sent back to his relatives in Chicago."

"You need me to help with those?"

"No, we don't need anything else from you. My grandmother

has agreed it's time you got out of Taos. We're taking you off the case."

"Off the case? Why?"

"Too many people are getting hurt. We don't want you to get killed, too."

"I can take care of myself."

Felicia snickered in the bathroom.

"That may be true," Ogletroop said, "but you haven't proven it so far. And, I assume you haven't discovered who murdered my sister?"

"Well, no. I've got some leads—"

"Just go home, Mr. Mabry. We'll be in touch."

The line clicked to dial tone before I took it away from my ear. "Damn!"

"What's the matter, honey?" Felicia called from the bathroom, as if she hadn't already figured out everything he'd said.

"The Ogletroops want me off the case."

"That's too bad. Does that mean you're going home today?"

"Yeah, I guess so. I don't know what else I would do."

She came out of the bathroom, wearing one of my dirty shirts. The tails hung down to her knees.

"Doesn't that shirt smell?"

She pulled the front of it up to her nose, took a whiff.

"It smells like you. I like that."

"Hmm. Maybe I'll stop showering."

"I don't like it that much."

She sat on the bed, curling her legs up under her.

"I think I'm going back to Albuquerque this morning, too," she said. "I've done about everything I can up here. I'll keep calling the sheriff. I can always zoom back up here if they find Margaret's killer."

I only half listened, too busy doing the math on the thousand-dollar retainer from the Ogletroops, trying to figure whether they'd demand any of their money back. Might be time to do some fancy bookkeeping on my expenses.

"Bubba? I said I'm going back to Albuquerque, too. Should we go together?"

"Oh, uh, no. I've got to get my car. And I need to make some phone calls."

Felicia rolled her eyes at my distraction.

"I can see we're not going to be playing any more patty-cake this morning," she said. "I might as well get dressed."

"What? Uh, no, don't do that. Climb back under the covers."

"Nope. Too late. I need a shower. Then I'll give you a lift to where you left your car."

She bounced out of the room, leaving me with my thoughts, which were vague and scattered, wispy clouds on the blank sky of my mind.

Off the case. Sure, I'd been yanked off cases before, usually by sighing clients who were tired of pouring money down a rat hole. But I'd really hoped to solve this one. I'd had high hopes for good publicity, for a change. I'd thought I might get in tight with the country club set, based on the Ogletroops' recommendation. Rich folks have lots of dirty secrets and plenty of money to have them cleaned up. And then there was Felicia. Impressing her was a big motivation in this case. Instead, she yanked my fat out of the fire. Once again, I proved a big disappointment to everyone, but mostly to myself.

When I heard the shower turn off, I forced myself out of bed and into some clothes. My hair was stiff and spiky from the night's sex sweat and I threw water on it until it calmed down. By the time Felicia emerged from the steamy bathroom, I'd packed my kit and was ready to go.

It didn't take her long to get ready. We threw our bags into her Toyota and drove back out toward WOMB. Felicia tried chatting, but she recognized quickly the conversation was one-sided and so she fell silent. I felt like an old rug on cleaning day, watered down and wrung out and all the grit beaten out of me.

She followed my directions to the Valdez ranch. The old man sat in his rocker on the porch. He stood and waved when he saw it was me.

"You can just let me out here," I said.

"Where's your car? I don't see it." Felicia eyed the old man suspiciously.

"It's up the way there in that pasture. Not too far of a walk. And I don't think your little car has enough clearance to manage that road."

"Okay." She sat still behind the wheel while I gathered my stuff, then leaned over for a kiss before I got out.

"Bubba? Don't take it so hard. They may never find out who killed Margaret. It's not your fault."

"I know. I just hate to leave a job unfinished."

"Sometimes, that's all you can do."

I remembered Reasons's words, how he'd said standing by and watching sometimes is all you can do. For some reason, it made me mad. I cleared my throat, tried not to let Felicia read my face. I told her good-bye, then strolled over to Jeronimo Valdez while she turned the car around and sped away.

He met me at the front stoop, squinting at the sunshine while he looked me over. He spat a stream of tobacco juice that missed my shoes by inches.

"When I said you could drive up into my pasture, son, I didn't expect a goddamn parade."

"What?"

"All those vehicles going in and out. I thought you said it would just be you and that other boy."

"You mean Reasons."

"Right, that was his name. Where is he, anyway?"

"Dead."

Valdez seemed unperturbed by this news. "Is that a fact? Why don't you have a seat and tell me all about it."

Another recounting was the last thing I wanted, but the old man had done me a favor. I could at least fill him in, keep him company. I sat in the straight-backed chair and he settled into his rocker.

"I'd offer you some coffee," he said, "but we're out. Juanita's gone into town to pick up some groceries."

"That's okay. It's getting too hot for coffee already, anyway."

That part was true. The temperature had to be in the eighties already and it wasn't even midmorning.

"So what happened to your partner?"

I ran it down for him, most of it, anyway. I figured the fewer people who knew about how Felicia and I escaped WOMB, the better. When I was done, he nodded and chewed, looking thoughtful.

"Your car's still up there," he said finally. "I saw it this morning when I drove out to check on a heifer. I wondered why you'd left it there."

"That's why I'm back up here today. I'm just getting the car; then I'm driving back to Albuquerque. No offense, but I've had about enough of Taos for a while."

He chuckled to himself, nodded some more. Just when I began to think he'd nodded himself into a nap, he spoke up.

"You don't know anything about those trucks, eh?"

"What trucks?"

"They followed you up here, I guess. Couple of them. I only saw one, but Juanita told me about another one a couple of days ago."

"What'd they look like?"

"Well, I only saw the one, like I said. Think it was a Ford, older truck, kinda gray, like it needed a paint job."

"It had ladder racks on the back?"

"That's the one. Somebody looking for you?"

"Yeah. That's the son of a bitch who killed Reasons."

Valdez took that in stride.

"D'you get a good look at him?"

"Pretty good. My eyes ain't what they used to be. I used to be able to count the legs on a flea at fifty paces. Now, I'm lucky to know a bull from a heifer."

"But you did see the driver?"

"Yessir. Young fella like yourself. Good-sized. Had a lot of hair, big bushy beard. Goddamn hippie."

"You talk to him?"

"Naw. I hollered over at him when he opened my gate, but he didn't even turn around."

"What day was that?"

"Well, I saw him twice. The first time was right after you boys showed up here that first day. What was that, Saturday?"

"Right."

"Then I saw him again, up on the pasture, guess it was Monday. I started driving my pickup over toward him, but when he saw me, he cranked his truck and drove away."

So the bastard had been following us the whole time, staking us out, waiting for a chance to sink an arrow into somebody's neck.

"What about the other truck?"

"Well, like I said, I didn't see that one. Juanita mentioned it to me. Some kind of fancy four-wheel drive, think she said it was red. But I don't know that for sure."

"And when was that?"

"Hmm." He pondered that for a minute. "Saturday? Sunday? I'm not entirely sure, but I think it was Saturday. I'd gone into town and she told me about it when I got back."

A red four-wheel drive? The Range Rover that Ogletroop drove was a sort of dark maroon. Maybe that's whom she'd seen.

But what would he have been doing up here?

"If it's who I think it was, it must've been on Sunday," I said.

Valdez squinted off at the horizon, trying to remember.

"Maybe it was," he said, "but I think it was Saturday. Stick around and you can ask Juanita about it. She'll be back before long."

"No, I think I'd better be going. The dead girl's family has ordered me off the case anyway, so it's not my problem."

"Whatever you say. I'm glad you stopped by. Gave me a chance to catch up on the coming and going around here."

"Well, you won't have to worry about any more of that. I don't ever plan to go back to WOMB again. You see anybody else poking around your pasture, you call the law."

"I'll fill 'em full of buckshot. That's the law up here."

I stepped down off his porch, trudged away toward the pasture. He was standing when I looked back from the gate, and we waved.

Once back in town, I found a pay phone and called Sheriff Hernandez. The woman who answered the phone demanded to know who I was before she'd put me through to the sheriff.

"Mabry!" he said when he came on. "Who's dead now?"

"Nobody. I'm dead tired. Does that count?"

"Join the club. Ever since you came to town, I haven't had a single good night's sleep."

"I'm about to fix that for you. I'm going home."

"Is that right?"

"Yes, sir. I've enjoyed as much of Taos as I can stand."

He chuckled.

"Well, that's about how much we've enjoyed having you."

"I'm sure."

"So," he said, "where do I reach you there?"

I gave him my phone number.

"You're not planning to take any trips or anything?"

"Not me. You'll be able to find me there if you need me. I'd appreciate it if you keep me posted on any developments."

That was greeted by a long silence. Finally, he said, "Why would I do that?"

"Maybe because I've played it straight with you. Maybe because you even like me a little."

"Don't push it, hotshot. You and I might've been buddies under some other circumstances, but right now you're just part of my workload. A big part."

"True enough. But you've played fair with me so far, and I appreciate it. I'll be talking to you."

"That's what I'm afraid of."

He hung up. I couldn't tell how much of his brusqueness was just hot air. I didn't care. I just wanted to go home.

I'd conveniently forgotten to tell the sheriff I was no longer working for the Ogletroops, or what Valdez had said about the trucks. He'd find it all out on his own soon enough.

I don't remember much about the drive back to Albuquerque. I was too busy thinking about old man Valdez's revelations, too busy stewing over being taken off the case. It's a wonder I didn't drive off the winding highway into the Rio Grande, so lost was I in my thoughts.

I hit a monsoon just south of Santa Fe, rain coming so hard that I pulled off the highway under an overpass to wait it out. It was late afternoon by the time I got home, where more bad news lay in wait for me.

T W E N T Y - T W O

■ ◆ ■

I hadn't gotten out of the car once on the way back, and I had a
bad case of creaky knees as I trudged into my room at the Desert
Breeze. The rain hadn't reached Albuquerque, and it was hot and
muggy. It was even hotter in my room, which had been shut up
for days.

I left the door standing open, threw my kit bag on the bed,
and put my gun in its usual drawer. I checked to make sure my
money and Kathy Grabow's check were where I'd left them. The
red light blinked on my answering machine, and I hit the rewind
button before heading off to the bathroom.

When I returned, I hit the play button and a breathless voice
filled the room: "Hello, Mr. Mabry. This is Kathy Grabow and,
uh, I've got some bad news. Marty found out about our little
setup. He saw where I wrote the check to you, and he demanded
to know who you were. . . ."

Beep! My machine, an older model, has a way of cutting people off in midsentence. Fortunately, she'd called back right away,
and hers was the next message, too.

"It's Kathy again. Your machine hung up on me. Anyhow, Marty called the bank and stopped payment on your check. He's really mad. I'm not sure what to do now. Call me."

There were other messages—one from Felicia, one from Marcus Ogletroop—but I barely heard them. That little shit! Stop payment on my check when I'd done the job as well as possible. I'd let him pop me upside the head, kick me in the belly. He'd gotten his money's worth. And now I've got nothing. A piece of worthless paper written for three hundred bucks, not even enough to take him to court over.

I dialed Kathy Grabow's number, which was on the check, and impatiently listened to it ring.

"Hello?"

"Mrs. Grabow? This is Bubba Mabry."

"Oh, Mr. Mabry. I've been wondering when I'd hear from you. I'm sorry for all the problems I've caused."

That velvety voice took some of the wind out of my sails. I'd been ready to yell and scream and stomp around in indignation, but I couldn't do that with her on the other end of the line.

"Is your husband home?"

"No, he's still at work. They're building an apartment building over on Montgomery Boulevard."

I asked for the address, and she gave it to me, then caught herself.

"You're not planning to go over there, are you? Marty's still steamed about you and the trick we played on him."

"I intend to get my money. Unless you want to bring it to me—cash—right now, then I'm going to see Marty."

"I'd love to, Mr. Mabry, but I promised Marty I wouldn't. He was so angry at me. He threatened to cut off my allowance if I misused any more of our money. I couldn't have that. I—"

"Bye, Mrs. Grabow."

I hung up on her, bounced to my feet, and headed for the door. I paused outside on the sidewalk, my hand still on the doorknob, thinking about whether to go back for my gun. The telephone rang, no doubt Kathy calling back, trying to talk me out of going to see her husband. Screw her. I slammed the door shut. I didn't need my gun for that sawed-off, wide-bottomed rich boy. He'd give me my money or I'd clobber him.

I drove too fast, going north on San Mateo to Montgomery, muttering and grinding my teeth. I'd had too many emotional ups and downs in the past few days for this little turkey to cross me now. I'd cream him. I'd maul him. I'd chew him up and spit him out. I'd tear off his head and piss down his neck.

The construction site covered nearly a city block, all ringed by chain-link fence. A big pit surrounded by pyramids of fill dirt covered the center of the lot, and a giant cranelike machine drove piles into the pit with a hammer the size of a car. The steady *boom-boom-boom* of the pile driver irritated me further. I swung the Chevy around the far side of the construction site and parked it among dusty pickups that must've belonged to the construction crew.

A gate stood open nearby, and I stalked through it, swinging my head back and forth, searching for Marty. A twenty-year-old with a ponytail and scraggly whiskers on his face spotted me and trotted over. He wore no shirt, and his lean body was darkly tanned. He had a yellow hard hat turned backward on his head and earplugs hanging on an orange string around his neck.

"Excuse me," he shouted over the noise of the pile driver. "This is a closed site. You can't come in here without a hard hat."

I waited until the next boom passed.

"I'm here to see Marty Grabow. Where is he?"

The youth took a step backward and glanced over his shoulder to where other hard-hatted crewmen stood around, leaning on shovels, watching the machine do the work.

"He's over there in the trailer. But you can't come in here without a hard hat."

"Fuck off."

I gave him a push in the chest as I went by. No reason for that. But I was too worked up now for any interference.

I stormed across the construction site toward the white mobile home that served as the office, kicking up dust as I went. The young worker doubtlessly was running over to tell his mates about the angry stranger on the site, but I didn't look over my shoulder toward them. I was too focused on getting a handful of Marty Grabow.

I didn't bother knocking. I shoved the door open and stepped inside. Marty stood facing me, leaning over a drafting table covered with blueprints, looking smart in fat-boy jeans and a white polo shirt. Beside him stood a greasy-maned, red-eyed monster wearing a black leather vest and no shirt to cover up the snakes and dragons and skulls that covered his thick arms. He had a ZZ Top beard that would've hung to his waist, but he had it loosely braided into a facial ponytail, clenched at the bottom by a blue rubber band.

"Well, looky here," Marty said. "It's the private dick. I figured you'd be around to see me."

"Damned right. I want my money."

"I don't owe you any money."

"The hell you don't. Your wife contracted for my services. I performed the services to her satisfaction. Pay me."

He looked me over, smirking, like he could bust out laughing any minute. That didn't make me feel any better. My breath was coming hard, and my fists clenched on their own accord.

"Looks like you still got something of a black eye there," Marty said.

"You son of a bitch, pay me now or—"

"Or what? You gonna pounce on me? I already whipped your ass once."

"I *let* you do that, pipsqueak. This time, it would be for real."

"Is that right? And you think Clyde here is gonna let you take a cut at me?"

I glanced over at the biker, who stood silently, the muscles in his arms flexing and rippling, giving the tattoos lives of their own. I've got a personal rule: Never argue with a man who has a tattoo. Somebody that impervious to pain is not the type to consider the consequences before acting.

"This is no business of his. You pay me, I'll go away quietly. You don't, and we're gonna have trouble."

Marty smirked some more. "I don't think so. I think you're going to get out of here now and leave us alone. We've got work to do."

Maybe I could trip him up. "You being paid for that work?"

"Sure."

"Then why shouldn't I be paid for mine?"

"Because what you did wasn't honest work. You tried to trick me. You conned my wife into going along."

"I conned nobody. She was trying to help you."

"I don't need that kind of help. And I don't need you coming around here disturbing my work site. Now get out."

"I'm not going anywhere until you pay me."

"Fuck you."

I stepped toward him, my hands curving into claws as I reached for his neck. He didn't startle. He just said, "Clyde."

The brute reached behind him, came up with a shiny eight-inch knife. It had a wicked curve to the blade. It looked sharp.

Clyde held the knife face-high, admiring its beauty, and said in a low, gruff voice, "Go away."

"You'd cut me just because this little shit said to?"

Clyde grinned, exposing crooked yellow teeth, and shrugged one shoulder. "He's the boss."

"I don't believe you'd do it."

I took another step toward Marty, saw the fear rise in his eyes as I got closer.

The knife suddenly appeared about an inch from the tip of my nose. Clyde leaned toward me. I could smell cigarettes on his breath.

"You'd better believe it, hoss. Now, shoo."

I backed away, my hands out to the sides, wishing I'd brought my trusty Smith & Wesson after all. When my back bumped the door, I reached behind me to fumble for the knob. Clyde closed in, the knife held comfortably at waist height, ready to disembowel me if I made the wrong move, said the wrong thing.

My bravado, what was left of it, made me try for the last word.

"You haven't heard the last of me, Grabow."

"Get him, Clyde."

I flung open the door and didn't bother with the steps down from the trailer. I landed on my feet, running before I hit the ground. Clyde bounded down the stairs behind me.

The construction crew had gathered outside, waiting to see what happened, and I blasted right through them, knocking one guy down with my shoulder, pushing others out of the way.

A general cry went up from the men, and they gave chase. I looked over my shoulder to see a dozen of them on my heels, some carrying wrenches or hammers or pieces of lumber, ready to brain me. The sight gave fuel to my feet, and I outdistanced them to where the cars were parked. I yanked my keys from my pocket when I reached the Chevy, climbed inside, turned the ignition. The engine coughed, making me catch my breath in terror; then it started, and I slammed the car into reverse and backed away at top speed just as the fastest of the workers reached my car. I wheeled the Chevy around, gunned it into the street without looking for traffic. The back tires slipped and the car fishtailed crazily for a second, then straightened out.

I rocketed past the construction site, back the way I'd come, but not so fast that I didn't get a final glimpse of Marty Grabow. He was standing on the trailer's stoop, his head thrown back, laughing.

TWENTY-THREE

■ ◆ ■

Humiliation is hard on a man, and I'd had more than my ration over the past few days. I spent the evening cloistered in my room, Jack Daniel's my only friend, engaging in that most male of activities: plotting revenge.

Women, faced with failure and embarrassment, focus on putting up a good front, appearing noble and optimistic. Men sink into a violent fantasy world, imagining all sorts of ways they could hurt or ruin or kill whomever they blame for their downfalls. And, there's nearly always someone else to blame. If I had to take full responsibility for all my failures, it would be too much of a load to carry. A man needs to spread it around.

I sat in my ratty old armchair, pouring down whiskey, thinking about how to get even with Marty Grabow. I could catch him alone somewhere and pound him. That would probably be the most satisfying answer. But it wouldn't be at the construction site, not with Clyde and the other loyal bruisers hanging around. Even with my gun, that would be too risky. Clyde looked like he could throw that knife through me and three walls without pulling a muscle.

Then I started putting together a team in my head, tough guys who owed me favors, men who could keep Clyde and the others at bay while I squeezed my money out of Marty Grabow. Guys like Johnny the Hook and Butch Mayfield and Tommy Wingnut and that old boxer, Dutch Murphy. They'd probably get a kick out of a rumble. Of course, if they knew there was money involved, they'd all want a cut. The favors they owed me weren't so impressive that they'd ignore a quick buck. Except maybe for Dutch. He just liked to fight.

Truth was, I didn't like to fight, didn't like to place myself in jeopardy. You can never tell when a lucky punch might send you to the undertaker. I remember, a few years ago, some kid whammed a hustler on the Cruise, just for the fun of it, and the old queen fell backward. His head hit a curb and the witnesses said it sounded like somebody'd dropped a watermelon. The kid, as I recall, ended up in maximum security up at Santa Fe. Wonder what he thinks about gays now that he's undoubtedly some con's girlfriend.

I tried to burrow out from under my bad mood. I tried to work out Reasons's murder and the Ogletroop case, but thinking about WOMB just reminded me of my recent humiliations and I was right back to mentally taking it all out on Marty Grabow.

By midnight, I was in an irritable stupor, and it was all I could do to get out of my clothes before I tumbled into bed.

I paid for all the drinking the next morning. It was late when I awoke, and the sun peeked through a crack between the drapes and hit me in the eyes like a laser beam. I covered my face with my hands, but then I could smell my own whiskey breath, and that was worse. I rolled up to a sitting position, and my brain caught up a few seconds later. Then I stumbled into the bathroom for aspirin and a toothbrush and a bath.

It was midday by the time I felt nearly human again. I tried not to think about Marty Grabow, tried to tell myself to write him off. He hadn't laid a glove on me this go-round, and my head still pounded. I'd done it to myself, through my own mean fantasies, my own weakness. Like my old mother says, You can't escape through the mouth of a bottle. It's too narrow. And drowning your troubles just irrigates them.

Kathy Grabow's check smirked at me from the bedside table. I snatched it up and crumpled it and tossed it in the wastebasket. Worthless paper now. No sense keeping it around to mock me.

The check reminded me, however, that I'd had other messages on my answering machine the night before, including one from Marcus Ogletroop. He probably wanted his money back, too. I sighed and dialed.

A chirpy maid with a strong Spanish accent answered, told me Marcus wasn't home. I asked to speak to Mrs. Ogletroop instead, and the maid replied in the cadence of a well-rehearsed line: "Mrs. Ogletroop is gravely ill and cannot be disturbed."

"Look, this is Bubba Mabry, the detective. Marcus left me a message yesterday. He wants to talk to me. Can't you tell me where I could find him?"

She thought it over.

"He's flying somewhere on business," she said. "That's really all I know."

"In his private plane?"

"Yes."

"Okay, I'll find him. Thanks a lot."

After I hung up, I had second thoughts about running Ogletroop down. I still felt like hell, I hadn't had anything to eat, and he couldn't have anything but bad news for me. Maybe I should just wait for him to get back to me. But the truth was, I didn't want to stay locked up in my room any longer. After everything I'd been through, you'd think I'd like to hide away, watch some TV, brood some more in the comfort of my own home. But my room felt small and stale after the wide open spaces of Taos. I needed to move, to do something other than drinking and beating myself up.

Albuquerque has only one place where private jets can comfortably take off and land: the general aviation area tucked in behind the main airport. Only a couple of outfits over there—Cutter Aviation, Executive Aviation—serve that clientele, so it wouldn't be too tough to track down Ogletroop's jet. And, if I missed him, I'd at least be out and about, and I could rustle up some lunch somewhere.

I drove south from Central until I hit Gibson Boulevard, the six-lane thoroughfare that borders Kirtland Air Force Base and Albuquerque International Airport, so close to the runways that they have shields to keep jet exhausts from melting the paint jobs of passing cars. I went west on Gibson to Yale, then swung south past the main airport to the low buildings that cater to the private planes.

A fat middle-aged guy at the Cutter counter eyed me suspiciously—Christ, I'd be glad when that shiner finished fading away—but finally told me Marcus and someone named Roy were doing their final checks out by the runway and that I could catch them if I hurried.

I trotted across the hot tarmac, my head pounding with every step, ducking under the wings and around the tails of tethered Cessnas and Pipers and Lears. I spotted Marcus up ahead, standing near the open door of a sleek white Learjet, checking his watch, holding one of those shiny stainless-steel briefcases in his free hand.

Another guy, potbellied and casual in a cowboy shirt and jeans, ducked under the nose of the plane and ambled around to Marcus as I loped up to them.

"Mr. Ogletroop!"

Marcus's head snapped up at his name and he looked annoyed to see me.

"Well, well, if it isn't the famous private eye."

That pulled me up short. I slowed to a walk, tried to catch my breath. It felt like someone was trying to pull my brain stem loose with a crowbar.

"I got your message," I said. "You needed to talk to me?"

"It wasn't urgent," Marcus said, checking his Rolex again. "I'm in a hurry now. It'll have to wait."

I gulped some more air. "I drove all the way out here. You couldn't just tell me what it's about?"

Marcus sighed, checked the sky. The other guy, who I took to be Roy, came up to stand beside him, checking out this stranger who was bothering the boss. Roy wore a baseball cap with some aviation fuel advertised across the front, and he had a lumpy nose. He looked familiar to me, but I knew I'd never met Marcus's pilot. I studied him more closely while Marcus Ogletroop whined about how he couldn't be late for some meeting in Phoenix.

I started at Roy's face and worked my way down, but it wasn't until I reached his feet that something clicked in my mind. He wore round-toed ropers, the same shade of blue as the cloudless sky above. I'd seen him before, all right. I'd seen him making a jackass of himself trying to two-step with every woman in the bar of the Sagebrush Inn, the night Margaret Ogletroop was killed.

I turned to Marcus, and he must've seen something in my eyes, because he stopped whining.

"I thought you were in Albuquerque when your sister was murdered," I said.

"What?"

"You spent the night in Taos, didn't you? You were there when word came that your sister was killed, and you let me believe you'd flown back up there to claim her body."

"What are you talking about?"

Roy suddenly had taken an intense interest in the ground at his feet. I knew I was right.

"Roy here flew you up earlier, isn't that right, Roy? Then you told him to keep quiet so no one would put you in Taos at the time of the killing."

Roy wouldn't look at me, but a flush spread over his jowly face. Marcus, on the other hand, looked stern and angry, creases between his eyebrows, his teeth clenched.

"I don't have time for this, Mabry," he spat. "You're crazy, and I'm late. Now get out of here. Crank her up, Roy."

Roy didn't move. I kept talking.

"I saw Roy last Saturday night, dancing at the Sagebrush Inn. He didn't see me. I was sitting in the back, nursing a drink, while he was dancing. But I recognize those boots, and I recognize him. If your pilot was already in Taos, he couldn't very well have flown you up there the next morning, could he?"

Marcus glanced around the airport, squinted up at the sun.

"I don't have to stand here and listen to this."

"You went up to WOMB Saturday in that maroon Range Rover I saw you in on Sunday. I have a witness who saw you up there, following my car. You stashed the Range Rover somewhere, waited for me to leave, then went down to WOMB and killed your sister."

"Now wait just a goddamn minute! You can't say that. That's slander! I'll have you arrested."

"I don't think you want to call the cops. Not right now. Not with Roy here as a witness."

Roy still studied his boots, as if cursing himself for wearing such noticeable footwear. Finally, he sighed and raised his head.

"He's right, boss," he said. "Maybe we ought to sort this thing out before it gets ugly."

"You shut up! You'll do what I say, or you'll be hunting another job. As for you, Mabry, you push me any further and I'll see to it that you never work again."

"Come on, boss," Roy said. "You didn't do anything wrong. Tell him about when we were up there. Sort it out."

Roy's eyes were pleading. He didn't want to believe his employer was capable of murder, or that he'd played a role in it. Hell, I thought, if he's been with the family long, he probably knew Margaret, probably flew her back and forth to Vassar.

"I said crank up that goddamn plane."

Roy shook his head slowly.

"Can't do it, boss."

Marcus sighed and his shoulders sagged. It took him a while, but he finally met my eyes.

"All right, all right. It was an accident, okay? I never, ever would've done anything to hurt my sister. She meant the world to me. But accidents happen and—"

"You killed her." My voice was low and hard, just enough of a prod to keep him talking.

"It wasn't like that, I tell you. I followed you, sure, but I didn't mean her any harm. I just wanted to talk some sense into her, to get her away from that cult before she gave away the family fortune."

"You found her by her shrine."

"Yeah, that's right. She was kneeling over those rocks, burning some smelly shit on a stick, chanting or something. I don't know. When I saw her, I couldn't control myself. I ran up to her and grabbed her by the shoulders and spun her around and started yelling into her face, telling her how she had to get out of there. She wouldn't do it. She told me I'd never understand her because I'm a *man*. I don't know what the hell that was supposed to mean. I sort of shook her, not hard—you know, just trying to shake some sense into her, but my . . . my hands slipped

182

and she fell backward and her head hit that slab of rock."

Roy was wide-eyed. He looked like a startled fish.

"I was horrified, of course." Marcus was practically babbling now that his cork had been popped. "I never intended for such a thing to happen. I checked her pulse, but I couldn't find it and she wasn't breathing. What was I to do? I had to try to cover my tracks and get the hell out of there."

Marcus's eyes had teared up, but I couldn't tell if he was crying for his sister or himself.

"So you laid her out on the slab and put a knife through her heart."

He wiped at his eyes with the back of his hand.

"Don't be so fucking flip about it," he said. "It was the hardest thing I've ever done. But I panicked, don't you see? If I was caught, everything would crumble . . . everything would be ruined. I wasn't thinking just about me. I was thinking about the business, about the hundreds of people we employ, what we mean to the community. All of that would come crashing down. The knife was right there—"

Roy finally erupted.

"My God, boss, I can't believe this. You told me you had nothing to do with Margaret getting killed."

Roy turned to me, jabbering. "I didn't know nothing about this. He told me we had to keep it quiet because it would raise questions if people found out we were up there—"

"Oh, shut up, Roy," Marcus snapped. "He knows you're not to blame."

He was right about that, but I wasn't finished. I took a menacing step toward Marcus.

"Then who did you hire to kill Reasons? Or were you trying to kill me?"

Marcus went wide-eyed, shook his head, pulled the briefcase up to cover his chest like a schoolgirl with her books.

"That wasn't me. I didn't have anything to do with that. I don't know who killed him."

"Come on, you can do better than that. You expect me to believe you now?"

"It's the truth. Sure, I was worried you and that damned nut would figure it out, but I didn't try to stop you. I didn't know what to do except to keep quiet and wait it out."

I didn't believe him. How could I? The man had proved himself capable of murder and deceit and God knows what other crimes. Killing Reasons and me would've completed the circle.

"Better lock up the plane, Roy," I said. "We're all going to go see the cops now."

Marcus's head snapped back and forth between Roy and me. A look of disbelief gripped his features.

"The cops? Are you crazy? Haven't you heard everything I just told you? They'll send me to prison. The newspaper will fall apart without me."

"That's too bad. You should've thought about that before you stuck that knife through her chest."

"But she was already dead! It was an accident!"

"If she'd already been dead, there wouldn't have been so much blood. Her heart was still pumping when you stabbed her."

That tripped Marcus up. He paused, his mouth hanging open, thinking about what I'd said.

Roy, nodding to himself, stepped behind Ogletroop, flipped a switch that caused the plane's door to rise slowly. It clicked shut, causing Marcus to whirl around.

"What are you doing? Open that door! We have business to attend to!"

"Not anymore you don't," I said. "Your only business now is with the law."

He swung back around, and I saw, too late, the steel briefcase was aimed at me. It caught me high on the side of the head, knocked me to my knees. I've never been shot in the head, but the sensation must be similar. My vision fogged and my hands splayed on the hot asphalt. I tried to shake it off before my face kissed the tarmac. I could hear Marcus's loafers slapping as he sprinted away.

I raised my head and, even though the world tilted crazily, I could see Roy hot on Marcus's heels, the blue boots clomping as they ran past the planes along the taxiway, toward the open ground of the runways.

"Boss! Boss! Come back!"

All that tennis had served Marcus Ogletroop well. His legs and arms were pumping. Roy was losing ground. I struggled to my feet, trying to help, but the steel briefcase had done me some damage. I couldn't seem to put one foot in front of the other. I stumbled over to the plane, caught myself against it with one hand, and watched the two men chasing away, Roy still shouting for Ogletroop to stop.

Then I heard another sound: a loud buzzing, like an angry wasp. It took me a second to locate it, but then I looked to the wide blue sky. A red-and-white single-engine plane was coming in for a landing, headed right toward the men as they sprinted onto the runway.

I tried to warn them. I screamed their names, but nobody could hear anything now except the whirring propeller. Marcus and Roy froze at the sound, then wheeled to their right just as the plane's wheels hit the concrete with a squeal. Roy, the aviation veteran, fell to his belly as if he'd been beaned by a fastball. Marcus stood frozen, his arms out to his sides, as the plane and its chopping propeller ran him down, sprayed him all over the runway.

TWENTY - FOUR

■ ◆ ■

Roy was about finished barfing by the time I staggered over to the runway. He was on all fours like a sick dog; I expected that any minute he'd start munching the sparse grass that grew alongside the asphalt.

The plane had come to a halt two hundred yards away. It taxied off the runway, and its door flew open and a skinny white-haired man clambered out.

Marcus Ogletroop's steel briefcase lay near my feet, spattered with his own blood. His crumpled body lay dead center in the runway, one leg bent back at a crazy angle. The propeller had hit him at least twice before the plane knocked him down. A pulpy red mass filled the space where his face should've been. A little fountain of blood danced from a huge gouge in his chest. As I watched, the blood pumped its last, trickled to a halt.

I'm always surprised by how much blood we all carry around inside us. Ogletroop's clothes were soaked and the tarmac all around him was splattered with red. I looked away, back toward the plane, and could see dots of red decorating its paint job and windshield. The white-haired man walked stiffly toward me.

In the distance, sirens screamed, coming closer. All my instincts said, Get the hell out of here. But running away was pointless, even if I'd felt clearheaded enough to make a break for it. The cops would be at my place before I could get there. And now, the white-haired pilot was approaching me.

"Goddamn it, man, what were you people doing on the runway?"

The old man seemed undisturbed by the blood all around. He just wanted someone to blame. He had a military bearing, his back as straight as a hoe handle, and I guessed he was one of the thousands of retired military officers who've settled in Albuquerque over the years. He'd probably seen worse than a single man chopped up and spread over a runway.

"It wasn't me," I said quickly, to divert him. "I was standing over there."

"You saw what happened?"

"More or less. Guy ran right out in front of you, right?"

"That's right." He seemed to calm a little, now that he had a witness. "I tried to pull the nose up, to get airborne again, but there wasn't time."

"Hey, I know," I said, playing along. "You're lucky the plane didn't flip or something, killing you, too."

"By God, I think you've got something there. I was so upset, I hadn't even thought about myself. I could've been killed."

Roy stumbled to his feet, wiping his face with his sleeve. The old soldier marched over to confront him.

The conversation was drowned out by the siren of the arriving ambulance. Two paramedics bailed out of the vehicle as soon as it screeched to a halt. They pulled up short when they saw Ogletroop's body. The younger of the two wheeled around, stepped off the tarmac, and threw up. Here's a boy, I thought, who needs to find another line of work.

The cops arrived seconds later. They questioned Roy and the old pilot. I hung around the edges of the ever-growing crowd on the runway. All the planes that would normally use the runway had been ordered to land elsewhere, I supposed. If another one was to land here now, a bunch of people might end up like Ogletroop, covered with a bloody sheet.

Roy told the cops about how I got a confession out of Ogletroop, and they waved me over. Before I started explaining it to them, though, an unmarked car rolled up, and Lt. Steve Romero climbed out.

Romero is an old pal of mine, though he might not describe us as friends. Our paths cross every so often, usually under unpleasant circumstances. He's the top investigator in the cops' Homicide Unit. I'm a little in awe of him. He's always tough and smart and wily. Being around him makes me feel like more of a doofus than usual.

The cops seemed to feel the same way. They parted for him to get into the thick of the crowd. He walked right up to me.

"Hi, Bubba, you taking an interest in aviation?"

"Naw, I just knew you'd be here and I love to see you in action."

Romero allowed himself a grin, clamped my arm in his thick hand, and walked me away from the others. The rest stayed where they were, watching Romero and me talk in low tones about what had happened. He had a notebook in his hand, but he didn't write much down. He just watched me with his sharp brown eyes, not missing a thing.

The more I talked, the more complicated the story got. After a while, Romero shook his head to stop me.

"We're going to have to go downtown," he said. "This is too much. We need you on tape."

"All right."

I followed him back over to the cops and the paramedics, who still clumped around Roy and the old pilot.

"You getting the statements from these other men?" Romero asked casually as we passed through them. The lead cop nodded. "Okay, then, get this mess cleaned up. The airport needs this runway open."

He was answered by a chorus of "Yes, sir" and we walked on over to his car. As I ducked into the passenger seat, I saw Felicia Quattlebaum and a *Gazette* photographer sprinting up to the scene. I waved, but I wasn't sure she saw me. She was too busy scoping out the carnage on the runway, writing rapidly in her notebook. I wondered whether she knew yet who lay under that sheet.

As we drove toward downtown, Romero said, "Bubba, you sure get yourself into some situations."

"Ain't it the truth? I don't go looking for trouble, but it always keeps on the lookout for me."

"So tell me again, how did you figure out Ogletroop killed his sister?"

"Boots. Blue boots."

Romero shook his head, tried not to grin.

"Never mind. It'll wait till we get to the office."

When we got there, it was hardly what you'd call a friendly conversation, though they did rustle up some aspirin for my pounding head. Romero, his hated boss, LeRoy Schulte, and three other detectives all crowded me into a small interrogation room on the fourth floor, and we went over the story again and again. Fortunately for me, Romero did most of the questioning. The others respected him enough to hold back, only occasionally asking for a clarification or for something to be repeated. Guess it was fortunate for them, too. Cops set off some sort of wisecracking compulsion in me. But not Romero. Not when he's serious. He's too crafty. I played it completely straight.

By the time we were done, I'd gone through the whole story—from the day the Ogletroops hired me until my arrival at the police station—four times. Schulte ordered one of the detectives to go call Sheriff Hernandez in Taos to confirm what I'd told them. When the detective returned, he gave a curt nod to the others.

The only hole in my story was the death of Purvis Reasons. Ogletroop had denied doing it before he died, and he wasn't around to ask again. Truth to tell, it didn't make any sense that he'd ordered Reasons killed. Or me either, if the man with the crossbow had been aiming at me. It wasn't as if we were about to expose Ogletroop's role in Margaret's murder. We didn't have a clue. I probably never would've stumbled over the truth if old Roy hadn't been such a feckless dancer.

Romero and the others weren't that interested in Reasons's murder, it turned out. It had occurred far from their jurisdiction. Ogletroop had died right here in town, and he was a big name locally. Once they were persuaded his death had been accidental, and that he was a killer besides, they turned me loose.

Romero walked me downstairs, not saying much. He looked a little weary, though nowhere near as tired as I felt. When we reached the lobby, where a security guard monitored all comings and goings, Romero clutched my arm.

"Let's take the back way out of here," he said. "There're too many reporters and photographers out there."

Sure enough, a cluster of them waited in the fading light outside. We could see them through the glass front doors, but they didn't spot us. They were too busy smoking and talking among themselves. I didn't see Felicia, but she no doubt was out there with the others, waiting for me.

Romero drove me back out to the airport to fetch the Chevy, a gesture I appreciated.

"That's all right," he said. "This way, I get to miss the press conference. Let Schulte take all the glory. That's all he's good for, anyway."

"How do you stand that rat-faced little shit? Why don't they put you in charge of Homicide?"

Romero smiled.

"Well, now, that's two decidedly different questions. I stand him because he's the boss and it's part of my job description to stand him. As for the second question, let me just say that I could probably have had the job, but I don't like pushing papers and kissing ass. Schulte's terrific at both those duties."

I smiled, for maybe the first time all day.

"Can I quote you on that, Lieutenant?"

"I'll call you a liar if you do."

He dropped me at my car, waved good-bye, then roared away. From where I stood, I couldn't see the spot where Ogletroop died, and I didn't bother going any closer. Seeing a man buzz-sawed by an airplane propeller would be hard enough to forget as it was. I climbed wearily behind the wheel, cranked up the Chevy, and drove home.

A light shone behind the curtains of my room. I parked the Chevy and slipped up to the door as quietly as I could. I hadn't left any lights on in the middle of the day, had I?

I pressed my ear to the door. Someone was talking inside, a woman's voice, and it took me a minute to recognize the voice as Felicia's. I pushed open the door. Felicia sat on my bed, her notebook in one hand, the phone in the other, haranguing some-body at the office. Her little computer sat on the nightstand in a tangle of wires.

"What are you doing here?"

"Gotta go," she said quickly into the phone, and hung it up without any niceties.

"How did you get in here?" Felicia had returned her key to my room when she moved out a year ago. I had tried to get her to keep it, but she didn't expect then to need it.

"Bongo let me in," she said. "I need to talk to you, and I knew you'd end up back here eventually."

"I'll have to have a talk with Bongo," I said. "I can't live someplace where the manager just lets people into my room when I'm not home."

She looked pained.

"Bubba, it's me. Bongo knows me. If I'd asked him to let me in, and he hadn't, you'd chew him out for that, too."

"You're right. I'm sorry. I'm just exhausted, and I'd hoped to tumble right into bed—alone."

She stood up and gathered me into a warm embrace. After the requisite pats and "poor baby"s she let me go and said, "Let me fix you a drink. Then you just sit down in that chair and sip some bourbon and tell me all about Marcus Ogletroop."

I didn't think I could bear to tell the story again, particularly when I knew it was all going straight into the newspaper, and I told her so.

"Sure you can," she said brightly. "Just one more time. Then I'll file my story and get out of here and let you rest."

What could I say? I sat. She brought the drink. I started talking. It turned out to be easier than I'd expected. Felicia already knew most of what had happened in Taos. The bourbon hitting my empty stomach was like grease on my talking gears. I spun it all out for her, then lay on the bed while she pounded away at her little keyboard.

By the time she'd transmitted the story to the paper, I was dozing. She kissed me on the forehead as she departed.

"You know," I said groggily, "I don't like to see my name in the paper. My cases are confidential."

She ran her fingers through my hair, patted my forehead.

"I know, Bubba. But you solved one. A big one. You should

192

take the credit. And think how impressed my parents will be when I show them the clippings."

Somehow, that made me feel a little better. I sighed once, and then was asleep. I didn't hear the door close behind her.

TWENTY-FIVE

■◆■

I read about Marcus Ogletroop's funeral in the Sunday *Gazette*. The funeral got a huge spread with color photos on the front page. Roy, the pilot, was in one of the photos, bawling like a newborn. Felicia was there, too; the story had her byline on it. I'd considered going, out of respect for Mrs. Ogletroop, but decided it would've been unseemly for me to show up. I was the guy who'd pegged him as a murderer.

From what I could tell from Felicia's story, the minister who ran the funeral had glossed over that little tidbit when he droned on about what an asset the community had lost in Marcus Ogletroop. Felicia, on the other hand, played up Margaret's murder big in her funeral story. I had to admit the *Gazette* surprised me. They hadn't flinched at showing the publisher's grandson for the scum he was. My admiration for the Goddess edged up another notch.

I'd kept to myself over the weekend. Felicia was busy anyway, cranking out one Ogletroop story after another. I tried to get my mind off the way Ogletroop had died. I did pretty well at it, busying myself with television and reading a cheap detective novel, but my mind betrayed me when I slept. I had strange dreams in which Margaret Ogletroop was the one who got sliced and diced by the airplane propeller. Reasons stood off to one side through each of the dreams, sometimes with the arrow protruding from his neck, looking annoyed with me.

On Monday, my phone rang bright and early, and I answered it from bed. It was Mrs. Ogletroop's nurse, Penny, who told me the old woman wanted me to come to her house. I could think of nothing I'd rather do less, but I felt I still owed something to the Goddess, so I told Penny I'd be there in an hour.

I didn't bother parking around the corner this time. Mrs. Ogletroop's impression of me was more likely to be shaped by her two dead grandchildren than by whatever I was driving. I parked the Chevy in the driveway, right outside the mansion's front door, got out, and rang the bell. The Hispanic maid opened the door and showed me in. I expected to be led back to the Goddess's bedroom again, but she surprised me by being in a drawing room just off the foyer, sitting up in a wheelchair.

She looked even paler and more drawn than before, but her posture was straight, and her silk bathrobe was immaculate. She shooed Penny out of the room with a wave of her gnarled hand, then ordered me to close the door and sit. I obeyed.

"Mr. Mabry." Her voice was thin, barely above a whisper. "I would imagine you're a bit uncomfortable, coming here to see me."

"You got that right, ma'am."

She smiled wanly, clutched her hands together in her lap.

"Don't be. I don't hold you responsible for Marcus's death. God knows, he had it coming to him after what he did to Margaret."

"I'm so sorry it all turned out this way, ma'am."

She clamped her lips shut as tears flooded her eyes. She waited a moment to regain her composure.

"So am I, Mr. Mabry, so am I. From the moment I learned of Margaret's death, I feared Marcus somehow was involved. The boy never was much good. He tried, I'll give him that, but he had a greedy streak he just couldn't overcome. I've watched him here the past few years, how impatient he was for me to die and get out of his way."

The speech seemed to drain her. She coughed a few times into a lace-trimmed handkerchief, swallowed, gasped for breath.

"Do you need me to get the nurse?"

"No, no, that's fine. There's nothing she can do for me."

I nodded, feeling my forehead crinkle in sympathy. Sometimes, I think I'd just as soon not get old. The way I live, the odds probably favor a short life, anyway.

"I called you here today," she resumed, her voice even softer. I scooted forward on the velvet divan, leaned toward her to hear. "I called you here because I wanted you to know I'm satisfied with the way you handled the job I gave you."

"You are?" That was the last thing I expected to hear.

"Yes. I put you and poor Mr. Reasons into a very difficult situation. Worse than I knew, really, when you consider what Marcus ended up doing. I hope the whole experience hasn't scarred you too badly."

My strange dreams flitted through my mind, but I shook my head.

"I've survived worse," I told her. "I'm not sure I have anyplace left where there isn't scar tissue already."

She nodded slightly, and rasped, "I meant scarring of the mental kind."

"So did I."

That made her smile.

"Well, then," she said, "I should let you go on about your business. I probably should rest before lunch."

"Yes, ma'am." I bounced to my feet and reached across to shake her hand, which was dry and cold and brittle.

"If it's not too much trouble," she said, "would you push my chair out into the foyer? I'd like to see you off."

I circled the chair, located the handles, and pushed. The chair rolled almost without effort. The Goddess was down to less than a hundred pounds. I rolled her out to a narrow window near the front door, parked her in front of it, set the brake. I saw Penny out of the corner of my eye, keeping a close watch from the hallway.

I had my hand on the doorknob, ready to go, when the Goddess said, "My goodness, is that your car out there?"

I felt a flush sizzle through my cheeks.

"Yes, ma'am. I've had that old Chevy for better'n ten years now."

"It looks like it's seen better days."

"That it has, but it still gets me where I need to go."

She nodded.

"Very well, Bubba. Good-bye, and good luck to you."

I trotted down the front steps, turned to wave at her. She was illuminated by the morning sun streaming through the window. She looked like a frail angel: white robe, white skin, white hair. It was almost as if the light penetrated her and lit her from within.

I climbed behind the wheel of the Chevy, muttering threats. Now that she'd noticed the car, I didn't want her to watch me crank at the damned balky starter for five minutes. The Chevy must've gotten the message, because the engine turned right over. I backed it out of the driveway and headed for home, carrying away the blessing of the Goddess.

TWENTY-SIX

■ ◆ ■

By late Monday afternoon, my own inactivity started to get to me. A man can only recuperate from an adventure for so long before he starts getting antsy about where he'll find his next dragon to slay—and his next paycheck.

I tried to call Felicia, whom I hadn't seen in days, but she wasn't home. Probably at the newspaper office again, uncovering some new crime. Maybe she'd figure out who killed Purvis Reasons, so I could stop fretting about it.

Just when I'd decided I had to get out of my room for a while, that I'd go hunt down Johnny the Hook and shoot some pool, the telephone rang. The phone had been the bearer of so much weirdness lately that I almost didn't answer it, but I couldn't stop myself in time.

"Hello?"

"Hello there, Bubba. This is Sheriff Hernandez, up in Taos County."

"Howdy, Sheriff. You're about the last person I expected to hear from today. I thought you'd had your fill of me."

"Well, that's true, I had. But now that you're gone, I confess I miss you a little. Nobody's been killed up here in nearly a week. It's getting boring."

I let that go. "What can I do for you, Sheriff?"

"It's more a matter of what I can do for you, I think. I've got some good news and some good news."

"A double helping of good news? I could sure use some of that. Bring it on."

"First off, you've probably forgotten that you've got a court date coming up for that trespassing charge. The good news is you won't have to drive all the way back up here. The charge has been dropped."

In fact, he was right: I had forgotten all about the charge pending against me.

"Did the WOMBsters decide they didn't have a case?"

"Oh, they had a case all right. Especially since I made the arrest myself. Saw you on their property with my own eyes. But Ms. Luna decided you'd suffered enough."

"Is that so?"

"We've been reading in the papers about that Ogletroop character, and working with the Albuquerque police to clear Margaret Ogletroop's murder from our files. I'm grateful for your help in the case, and I think Ms. Luna was, too. They'd felt bad 'cause people thought they'd killed one of their own.

"Plus, Ms. Luna told me about the little prank she pulled on you and that reporter. She felt like that was payback enough."

"Prank?" In times of great embarrassment, it's natural to play stupid.

"Whew, boy, I'd have given a hundred dollars to see the look on your face when you thought they were going to castrate you."

I felt myself smiling tightly into the phone.

"They've already done me enough damage," I said. "By telling you about it."

"Aw, now, don't take it so hard. I'm not spreading it around. Though it's one heck of a funny story."

"It didn't seem so funny at the time."

"I'll bet it didn't!" I heard him cup his hand over the phone as his laughter exploded forth. After a few seconds, he got hold of himself and continued.

"Seems Ms. Luna and the others were onto your reporter friend as soon as she arrived at WOMB. She parked her car down by the road there, and it was full of reporter's notebooks and cameras and stuff. Pretty clear what she was up to. Then, when they connected her to you, it only made sense for them to scare both of you off at once."

"It worked. I'll give 'em that."

Hernandez guffawed, coughed, cleared his throat. I could practically hear him wiping the tears from his eyes. It's a good thing I don't know how to fly an airplane. I would've dropped a bomb on WOMB.

"Anyhow," he said, "the charges are officially dropped."

"I don't suppose it occurred to you to file charges against them? Unlawful imprisonment, something like that?"

"Well, now, I guess we could file such a charge. But you'd have to come up here and swear out a complaint and testify in court about what they did to you."

"Never mind."

Hernandez laughed again. This sounded like the best time he'd ever had. I could just picture him: leaning back, his boots up on his desk, har-harring his afternoon away.

"You said there was more good news?" I asked abruptly, trying to steer him back on course. I heard his chair squeak as he sat up to consult the mound of papers on his desk.

"Oh, yeah, that's the best part, at least from your viewpoint. We found your truck."

"My truck?"

"The one with the ladder racks? Shot your buddy with an arrow?"

"Really?"

"Yeah, it was down in an arroyo, about a hundred yards off the highway, up toward Questa. Somebody burned it, but it still had the ladder racks, so we figure it must be your boy."

"When was this?"

"Yesterday."

"Did it still have license plates?"

"Naw, whoever burned it wasn't that dumb. But they were dumb enough to leave the vehicle identification number in the dash. Those little VINs are hard to pry out of there. Whoever did it probably figured the fire would take care of it."

I took a deep breath, blew it out. Now was the time for the big question, the one that had me stumped.

"Who owned the truck?"

"Well, it's registered to a man down there in Albuquerque, a Mr. Clyde Purdy."

Clyde. Of course.

I said quickly, for Hernandez's benefit, "Never heard of him."

"Me neither. I sent the APD hustling over to talk to Mr. Purdy, but he claims the truck was stolen a week ago, and he hasn't seen it since."

"Had he filed a stolen-car report?"

"In fact, he had. Last Tuesday, the day after Mr. Reasons was killed."

"So, he had time to ditch the truck and report it stolen after he shot Reasons with that crossbow."

"It would seem that way, but APD says he's got an airtight alibi that puts him in Albuquerque the whole time. His boss and coworkers say he never left town."

"Is that so? Maybe I'll question Mr. Purdy myself."

"I'd advise against that. APD says he's a pretty rough character."

"To me, he's just another dragon."

"Huh?"

"Never mind. So long, Sheriff."

T W E N T Y - S E V E N
■ ◆ ■

Clyde Purdy was listed in the phone book, which made hunting him down pretty dang easy. The address led me to a tiny flat-roofed house just north of Interstate 40, well within reach of the roar of the freeway traffic. The house was in as much disrepair as Purdy's truck had been: The dark brown shingles that covered the exterior were peeling away, the yard was bare dirt decorated with trash and old hubcaps, and the one old tree out front was dead and spooky-bare. A big black Harley was parked on the front sidewalk, just outside the door. The gravel driveway was empty except for oil spots the old truck had left.

I parked down the street half a block, checked to make sure my Smith & Wesson was fully loaded, and clipped the holster to my belt, under my shirttail. Then I walked toward the house, searching for any sign of life.

The side yard was a jumble of weeds surrounded by a six-foot chain-link fence that came right up to the sidewalk. I about jumped out of my skin when a muscular pit bull sprang from the weeds, growling and snapping at me. He pressed his ugly, dripping face against the fence, as if he was trying to push through one of the diamond-shaped holes so he could get at me. No reason to be afraid of him, with the fence to protect me, but his barking would surely alert Clyde. I leaned over and spoke to the dog in a clear, calm voice.

"Shut up or I'll shoot you."

The dog must've heard that threat before, because he tucked his tail between his legs and, with a whimper, trotted away into the weeds. Somehow, a dog that smart didn't make me feel any better about what else I'd find at this house.

I walked into the bare front yard, slipped up to the nearest window. I couldn't see a thing. The window was curtained by a bedsheet that must've once been white but now was a sort of an awful beige, bearing so many stains that it looked tie-dyed. The window on the other side of the front door was covered the same way. Nothing to do but knock.

A gruff voice shouted something I couldn't make out from inside. I heard heavy footfalls approaching the door, and my hand drifted back to the butt of my pistol. The door swung open and there stood Marty Grabow's man Clyde in all his hairy, tattooed splendor.

"Hello, Clyde."

Clyde said nothing, just growled like his bad dog. He was shirtless, wearing only faded jeans and battered motorcycle boots, but he had his knife. He reached behind his waist, whipped out the big shiny blade. I came up with my pistol just as quickly. It was like that kid's game, scissors-paper-rock.

"Uh-uh-uh. I've got you outmatched here. I win."

"Bullshit."

He kicked me, quick and dirty, the big steel-toed boot crunching my fingers where they gripped my gun. The pistol went flying, bounced off the door, skittered across the dirty linoleum floor.

"Uh-oh." I turned to run, but Clyde grabbed me by the collar, dragged me inside, kicked the door shut.

He pressed the knife against my throat from behind. The steel felt cold against my skin.

"I've already had a shave today. Thanks anyway."

"Wiseass," he grunted. "I should've finished you up in Taos."

He hooked his thick arm around my neck and dragged me backward, farther into the narrow living room. The knife was by my ear. My feet couldn't keep a purchase on the slick floor, though they scrabbled and kicked on their own accord. Clyde growled and muttered into my ear. His skin felt hot against mine. He smelled bad, like sweat and oil.

Somebody's holding a knife near your neck, has got you in a good solid grip, probably the best thing to do is to go limp. Maybe he'll lose interest, like a cat with a dead mouse. Or, maybe, you should try to talk him out of killing you. But Clyde seemed intent on taking me out behind his house and doing me there. And he wasn't a good listener.

All I could see as Clyde dragged me along was the leak-stained ceiling and the wood-paneled walls. The walls were covered with an arsenal hanging on pegs: shotguns and pistols and rifles, swords, and, Christ, a crossbow. Clyde, it seemed, was a collector, and the weapons weren't just for show. The sight of the crossbow did something to me. Made me mad, in both senses of the word. I went crazy.

With death as close as that silver blade by my ear, I got my feet under me and lunged backward. It caught Clyde off guard, and the top of my head smashed into his chin. Then I swung an elbow back sharply, cracking him in the ribs. It sounded like someone striking a drum, and Clyde's foul breath oofed out of him. He let go of me, and I fell to the floor.

It didn't take him long to recover. He slashed the air near my head as I rolled away, then came after me with the knife as I scrambled to get my feet under me. I needed an equalizer, but he wasn't giving me time to find my gun or snatch one of his off the wall. The door was somewhere behind me, but I knew that knife would be between my shoulder blades before I could turn the doorknob and bolt.

I grabbed the only thing handy, which was a heavy glass ash-tray sitting on a table against the wall, and launched it toward his head. He ducked just in time and the ashtray whizzed past his head, scattering butts and ashes through his thick hair.

"Aaargh!" He charged me, knife leading the way. At the last second, I fell sideways, caught myself on the wall. My left leg was still extended, and he tripped over it, went tumbling down the short hall toward the front door, trying to find his balance.

Recognizing this was my only chance, I clambered to my feet and grabbed the nearest weapon off the wall, a sawed-off double-barrel shotgun. By the time Clyde turned to face me, I had both hammers cocked back.

"Now," I said, my breath coming hard, "drop that knife. We've got some talking to do."

He laughed at me—"Heh-heh-heh"—then came at me with the knife.

"You're asking for it." My final warning.

He kept coming.

I pulled the double triggers, wincing against the expected kick of the shotgun. *Click-click.* The gun wasn't loaded.

He was almost upon me. I turned the gun sideways in my hands and threw it at his face. He tried that ducking maneuver again, but he wasn't quick enough this time, and the heavy gun bounced off his cranium. He didn't even blink. In fact, he smiled, showing his yellow teeth. He looked like he wanted to bite me.

I backpedaled into the living room, searching for another weapon, something that didn't need bullets. My eyes settled on a half a dozen swords arranged on the wall and I made for them, but Clyde saw what I was up to and lunged across the room to cut me off. He slashed at me with the knife, but I was already backing away, and all he got was shirt. Still, that was too close. The sudden breeze around my chest where the shirt was slashed open gave energy to my feet. I danced backward, then raced around a sofa that sat in the middle of the room, pushing lamps and tables onto the floor behind me.

Clyde followed, which was just what I wanted. When the sofa was between us, I sprinted for the swords.

He leaped over the back of the sofa, bounced off the cushions, and launched himself toward me. But by the time he closed the distance, I'd snatched a saber off the wall and wheeled toward him.

He tried to pull up, tried to stop, but the motorcycle boots couldn't get a grip on the linoleum floor, and Clyde, with his arms wheeling, fell full force on the sword. I lost my grip on it as we crashed together against the wall. His knife missed my rib cage by inches, stuck in the paneling.

Then Clyde relaxed all over, slumped against me, his sweaty shoulder smashing my nose. I'd closed my eyes during the collision, and I opened them now, to see the red-streaked blade jutting from his bare back.

I slid sideways to get out from under him, let him fall to the floor. The sword must've gone right through his heart, because he was pumping out a geyser of blood. The front of my shirt was soaked with it.

I stumbled over to the sliding glass doors that led to his backyard and blew lunch all over the bare dirt out there. The pit bull watched me from behind a gate, licking his chops and whining.

When I finished heaving, I went back inside, to find Clyde the way I'd left him, lying on his side, the sword through his body. I looked away, swallowing bile, thinking, Live by the sword . . .

I located the bathroom, stripped off my bloody, ripped shirt, and washed my face and hands and arms in the yellowed basin. I could smell myself now, and the odor was as bad as Clyde's, a sweat composed of equal parts exertion and fear and last night's bourbon.

A black T-shirt hung on a peg on the back of the bathroom door. It had a screaming eagle and a Harley logo across the back, but it was better than walking out of Clyde's house half-naked. I slipped it over my head.

I walked out through the living room, trying not to look at Clyde lying there in his own blood, and searched under furniture until I came up with my pistol. Then I showed myself out. I had another stop to make.

T W E N T Y - E I G H T
■ ◆ ■

I scarcely remember driving to Marty Grabow's house. I know
the sky had begun its daily sunset show, scudding clouds lit un-
derneath with orange and pink and purple. The traffic still was
thick as I raced along Tramway Boulevard, the wide thoroughfare clogged with rich folks hurrying home from their workdays.
I located the Grabows' street in Sandia Heights, followed it as it
climbed and pitched into the foothills.

I slowed at the top of a hill when I spotted the house, a huge
white stucco Mediterranean with a red tiled roof. From up there,
I could see the whole spread, including the swimming pool out
back. By the pool was the dumpy figure of a man, who was ges-
ticulating at a blonde who lay back in a chaise longue. Just the
folks I was looking for.

I parked out front, pushed the Chevy's door closed without a
sound, and trotted around the house to the back. The pool area
was surrounded by a plank fence that was much higher than it
had seemed from up on the hill. I peeked between redwood
planks until I was sure I was between the Grabows and the house,

then grabbed the top of the fence and hauled myself over.

"What the hell?" Marty's voice. The chaise creaked as Kathy sat up to see.

I landed on my feet, facing them.

"Mr. Mabry?" Kathy still had trouble believing her eyes. Marty had no such trouble, instantly puffing up.

"Get off my property!"

"Shut up, Grabass." I pulled out my gun, pointed it their way. They clammed.

The pool was wide and deep and its ripples reflected the orange sky. The deck that surrounded it was made of pale red flagstones set into white mortar, so the whole thing resembled a giant raw steak. Potted evergreens sat along the fence. No furniture other than Kathy's chaise longue and a little glass-topped table that sat beside it. The table held up a cordless phone and a pink drink with an umbrella in it.

Marty held a tumbler of what looked like Scotch in his hand, and he glanced down at it, weighed it as a weapon.

"Set that down on the table." He did it.

Now that I had the situation scoped out, I could take a minute to look at the Grabows. Marty had on a dark green polo shirt that stretched tightly over his gut, baggy gray slacks, and work boots. And Kathy, oh Kathy, wore a white one-piece swimsuit that barely covered the required areas. I've seen lobster bibs that had more fabric. She clearly hadn't been swimming. Her blond hair was dry, her mascara unsmeared. The makeup made her eyes look even wider as she stared at me in disbelief.

Her husband huffed and puffed, mad about me showing up.

"I told you, I'm not paying you that three hundred bucks!" he shouted. "You'd better get off my property before I call the cops!"

I let him yell himself out, then said quietly, "I think *I'll* be the one who calls the cops."

210

"What?"

"I'm sure the cops want to hear all about how you sent Clyde up to Taos after me."

Kathy gasped, turned to look at her husband.

"What is he talking about, Marty?"

"I don't know. The man's crazy. You've gotten us mixed up with a crazy man."

"No, Marty, you're the one who got mixed up with the wrong man," I said. "Clyde was crazy. And now he's dead."

"What? I don't believe you!"

I half turned so he could see the eagle on the back of the T-shirt.

"Recognize this shirt? I took it from his house because mine was soaked with blood. It still smells like him. You can probably get a whiff of it from over there."

Even though he was ten feet away, Marty sniffed the air on command.

"I don't smell anything."

I sighed, lowered the pistol. My arm was tired. In fact, I was tired all over. I wanted just to go home and go to bed, but I had some settling up to do with Marty Grabow, and it wouldn't wait. If he had a chance to get to his lawyers and make his deals with the cops, I'd never get the full story. But he was such a hot-headed, hopped-up little guy, I couldn't get him to focus on what I was telling him.

I closed the distance between us, put the gun in his face.

"How about now? You believe me now?"

He gulped. Kathy stood up from her chaise, her hands clutched together near her breasts.

"Sit down," I said over my shoulder. She sat.

"Now, listen, limp dick. We're going to talk about Taos, and you're going to cooperate."

"I'll do no such thing. I know my rights—"

I grabbed his arm, swung around, and threw him into the pool. He made a huge splash, came up sputtering.

"That cool you down some? Now climb out of the water and talk to me."

He paddled over, hefted himself up onto the side of the pool, grunting. He stood up, water flying everywhere, and wiped his face with his wet hands.

"Can I give him a towel?" Kathy's voice came from behind me.

I took two steps backward. "Toss it over to him. Don't stand up."

It wasn't much of a throw. The towel landed near Marty's feet, and he bent to pick it up without taking his eyes off me, bowing like a suspicious karate master.

He dried off his face and hair, draped the towel around his neck.

"Mr. Mabry, if I'd known you were this kind of a man, I never would've hired you."

Kathy had summoned up all her inner reserves to make that little speech. I ignored her. She pouted.

"Okay, Marty, let's have it. Start with the part where you sent Clyde looking for me."

He glared at me, clamped his mouth shut.

"You want to go for another swim? I've got nothing else to do this evening. I can throw you in that pool all night. Or, I can start shooting holes in you. Imagine what the pool man will think when he comes to clean up the mess."

He thought it over.

"Clyde's dead?" he said finally.

"Yeah, he's dead. He's lying on the floor of his house right now with a sword through his heart. You still think I'm not serious?"

Marty's eyes widened. He clearly had seen Clyde's collection of swords. I spared him the details that Clyde had fallen on the sword himself, that I'd been lucky to walk out of there alive.

Marty sighed, glanced up at the darkening sky, the mountains that towered over his mansion.

"All right, all right," he said. "I sent Clyde looking for you after I learned you and Kathy had tricked me."

"And Clyde somehow figured out I'd gone to Taos."

"Yeah, he talked to somebody at that sleazy motel where you live, got a tip. I told him to go on up there after you, that we'd cover for him at work."

"And what did you tell him to do when he found me?"

"Scare you. I wanted you to feel some of the fear I'd been going through. But I didn't tell him to hurt anybody. Just to scare you."

"How'd he find me up there?"

"I don't know. I guess he spotted your car or something. He called me, said he'd located you, that he would take care of things. I didn't know what he was going to do. I didn't think about it much."

"When did you talk to him again?"

"He called me a couple days later. Told me he put a rubber snake in your bed. I liked that."

"I'll bet you did. That wasn't enough of a scare for you?"

"It would've been enough for me. But I could tell Clyde was getting into it. He was having fun, and it's not a good idea to stop Clyde when he's having fun."

"Yeah, well, he won't be having any more fun. He's too dead. Just like my partner, the one he killed up in Taos."

"I didn't know anything about that. Really. I didn't know Clyde would hurt anybody."

"Come on, the man was a freaking time bomb."

"He was a little dangerous, sure, but I thought he'd reel himself in before anybody got hurt. He told me, after he got back to Albuquerque, about how your friend got hit with that arrow. He

213

wasn't aiming for him. He was just trying to scare you. But, you know, Clyde was shooting from a moving truck. It was an accident."

"An accident?"

"More or less, yeah. I mean, he wasn't trying to kill that guy. It's just one of those things. Like when the weather ruins a construction job. In my business, it's called an act of God."

I squinted at him. I was finding it very hard to contain myself. The snotty little man should be pistol-whipped, at least. Other options wheeled through my head. Shoot him where he stood. Burn his house to the ground. Instead, I just sighed.

"I'm getting tired of people talking to me about 'accidents,' " I said. "It was murder, plain and simple. And you're an accessory. I think it's time to call the cops."

I stepped over to Kathy Grabow, picked up the cordless phone, dialed the police department.

"I can't believe this, Marty," she said. "I can't believe you got mixed up in something like this. You've ruined our lives."

Marty ignored her, too busy talking to me. "Hey, c'mon now. No reason to call the cops. We can settle this some way. I'm a rich man. What do you want? Money? You want a job? I could set you up for life. You wouldn't have to lift a finger. Just collect a paycheck every week."

I kept the phone to my ear, pointed the gun at him. "Shut up or I'll shoot your face off."

"C'mon! Let's talk about this—"

I pulled back the hammer on my pistol, and the click echoed around the pool. Marty ran out of words, hung his head.

"Oh, Marty, I'm so ashamed of you." Kathy shook her head, looking ever sadder. Too bad about her, I thought. She had everything she wanted, just by marrying the rich wimp. She started all this, trying to make her man whole again, and now she'd lose everything.

The cop shop finally answered and I asked for Lt. Steve Romero. Lucky for me, he was still in the office, working late. I briefly ran down the situation for him, and he said he'd send the cavalry.

Marty paced alongside the pool while we waited for the black-and-whites to arrive. The only time he spoke, he asked whether he could call his lawyer. In answer, I tossed the cordless phone into the pool.

After that, the three of us waited silently for the cops. Kathy Grabow dabbed at her eyes; the tears finally had broken through, streaking her cheeks with black. The sight of her weeping seemed to subdue Marty. He stopped pacing, stood helpless, watching her.

As we heard the sirens approaching, I stepped over to him. Hate burned in his eyes, but he said nothing. I shifted my gun to my left hand.

"I still owe you something," I said.

Then I cracked him hard as I could with my fist, right on the eye socket. The blow knocked him backward into the pool. It was several seconds before he broke the surface, gasping for air, long enough for Kathy Grabow to jump to her feet in horror. She leaned over to give him a hand, and I admired her behind while she hoisted him onto the side.

Marty clutched at his face like I'd shot him, lying there beached on the flagstone deck.

Kathy wheeled on me. "Why did you do that?"

"Just call it three hundred dollars' worth of satisfaction."

E P I L O G U E
■ ◆ ■

Weeks have passed. I was exonerated in Clyde Purdy's death. The district attorney ruled it a clear case of self-defense, even though I'd gone to Clyde's house looking for trouble.

Marty Grabow and his lawyers still are fighting the accessory charges, but it looks like he'll do time. I've stayed away from the courthouse except when I testified. The rest of the time, I watch it on the TV news. Marty's shiner looked real fine in living color the first couple of weeks.

While the local media chased Grabow from one courtroom appearance to the next, the national media descended on Albuquerque in pursuit of more on the Ogletroop story. I've refused to talk to all of them, giving Felicia the exclusive story. Slimy movie-of-the-week producers waved money under my nose, trying to get me to tell all about the Ogletroops, but I figured I owed it to the family to turn away all offers. It's been tempting, though. I've run through all the money the Goddess paid me, and I'm back on the street, running down little stakeout jobs to keep alive.

Things are back to normal between Felicia and me. Her parents came out from Indiana to visit, and it went off without a hitch. I looked like a big-shot private eye, what with my name in the newspaper in connection with two different investigations. And Felicia's dad turned out to be a regular guy. We even hoisted a few brews together over at Sonny's Lounge. For a geezer, he shoots a mean game of pool.

Despite all my exposure to WOMB, I don't understand women any better than I did before. Felicia says it's natural, that the more men and women become alike in society, the more we'll be puzzled by the differences between us. Seems to me that no matter how society changes, we'll always be governed by biology, by hormones. We'll never completely understand each other unless we're all willing to become eunuchs. And, having come close to that myself, I can vouch for the fact it's not worth it. A little mystery about the opposite sex probably is a good thing.

Mrs. Ogletroop passed away a couple of weeks after her grandson got chewed up by that plane. I hated to see her go. Apparently, a lot of people felt that way. The funeral was one of the biggest in the city's history. Congressmen, the governor, the mayor, and all the other muckety-mucks turned out for it, trying to get in good with the out-of-town nephew who inherited the newspaper. I didn't go. I would've liked to have paid my respects to the old woman, but the news media were there in force and they would've swooped down on me. Besides, I don't own a necktie. Saying good-bye to the Goddess was a formal event.

She said her farewell to me a couple of weeks later. A bland pinstriped lawyer showed up at my door, told me Mrs. Ogletroop had left me a bequest in her will. Then he led me out into the parking lot, where he presented me with a brand-new cherry red Dodge Ram pickup truck. It's a heck of a truck, with wide, sloping fenders and fat tires and a high chrome grille that makes it look like a Kenworth sixteen-wheeler. About as subtle as a fire engine. The last thing in the world I need for tailing people.

I thought about trading it in for something less conspicuous, maybe making a little money on the deal. But Felicia loves the truck. She likes sitting up high in traffic, her elbow draped out the window, riding with me along the Cruise.

Besides, she says, Mrs. Ogletroop knew what she was doing when she left me such a fine truck to replace my decaying Nova. You don't question a gift from the Goddess.